RA653.5 .P367 2008

Pandemics

Writing the Critical Essay

Pandemics

An OPPOSING VIEWPOINTS® Guide

Other books in the Writing the Critical Essay series are:

Writing the Critical Essay

Pandemics

An OPPOSING VIEWPOINTS® Guide

Lauri S. Friedman, *Book Editor*

OPPOSING VIEWPOINTS® SERIES

GALE
CENGAGE Learning

Detroit • New York • San Francisco • New Haven, Conn • Waterville, Maine • London

Christine Nasso, *Publisher*
Elizabeth Des Chenes, *Managing Editor*

© 2008 Greenhaven Press, a part of Gale, Cengage Learning

Gale and Greenhaven Press are registered trademarks used herein under license.

For more information, contact:
Greenhaven Press
27500 Drake Rd.
Farmington Hills, MI 48331-3535
Or you can visit our Internet site at gale.cengage.com

For product information and technology assistance, contact us at

Gale Customer Support, 1-800-877-4253
For permission to use material from this text or product, submit all requests online at www.cengage.com/permissions

Further permissions questions can be emailed to permissionrequest@cengage.com

Articles in Greenhaven Press anthologies are often edited for length to meet page requirements. In addition, original titles of these works are changed to clearly present the main thesis and to explicitly indicate the author's opinion. Every effort is made to ensure that Greenhaven Press accurately reflects the original intent of the authors. Every effort has been made to trace the owners of copyrighted material.

Cover image © Gideon Mendel/Corbis

LIBRARY OF CONGRESS CATALOGING-IN-PUBLICATION DATA

Pandemics / Lauri S. Friedman, book editor.
    p. cm.—(Writing the critical essay, an opposing viewpoints guide)
    Includes bibliographical references and index.
    ISBN 13: 978-0-7377-4039-4 (hardcover)
    ISBN 10: 0-7377-4039-6
    1. Epidemics--Juvenile literature. 2. Communicable diseases—Juvenile literature. I.
Friedman, Lauri S.
    RA653.5.P367 2008
    614.4—dc22   2008009024

Printed in the United States of America
1 2 3 4 5 6 7 12 11 10 09 08

CONTENTS

Examining the state of writing and how it is taught in the United States was the official purpose of the National Commission on Writing in America's Schools and Colleges. The commission, made up of teachers, school administrators, business leaders, and college and university presidents, released its first report in 2003. "Despite the best efforts of many educators," commissioners argued, "writing has not received the full attention it deserves." Among the findings of the commission was that most fourth-grade students spent less than three hours a week writing, that three-quarters of high school seniors never receive a writing assignment in their history or social studies classes, and that more than 50 percent of first-year students in college have problems writing error-free papers. The commission called for a "cultural sea change" that would increase the emphasis on writing for both elementary and secondary schools. These conclusions have made some educators realize that writing must be emphasized in the curriculum. As colleges are demanding an ever-higher level of writing proficiency from incoming students, schools must respond by making students more competent writers. In response to these concerns, the SAT, an influential standardized test used for college admissions, required an essay for the first time in 2005.

Books in the Writing the Critical Essay: An Opposing Viewpoints Guide series use the patented Opposing Viewpoints format to help students learn to organize ideas and arguments and to write essays using common critical writing techniques. Each book in the series focuses on a particular type of essay writing—including expository, persuasive, descriptive, and narrative—that students learn while being taught both the five-paragraph essay as well as longer pieces of writing that have an opinionated focus. These guides include everything necessary to help students research, outline, draft, edit, and ultimately write successful essays across the curriculum, including essays for the SAT.

Using Opposing Viewpoints

This series is inspired by and builds upon Greenhaven Press's acclaimed Opposing Viewpoints series. As in the parent series, each book in the Writing the Critical Essay series focuses on a timely and controversial social issue that provides lots of opportunities for creating thought-provoking essays. The first section of each volume begins with a brief introductory essay that provides context for the opposing viewpoints that follow. These articles are chosen for their accessibility and clearly stated views. The thesis of each article is made explicit in the article's title and is accentuated by its pairing with an opposing or alternative view. These essays are both models of persuasive writing techniques and valuable research material that students can mine to write their own informed essays. Guided reading and discussion questions help lead students to key ideas and writing techniques presented in the selections.

The second section of each book begins with a preface discussing the format of the essays and examining characteristics of the featured essay type. Model five-paragraph and longer essays then demonstrate that essay type. The essays are annotated so that key writing elements and techniques are pointed out to the student. Sequential, step-by-step exercises help students construct and refine thesis statements; organize material into outlines; analyze and try out writing techniques; write transitions, introductions, and conclusions; and incorporate quotations and other researched material. Ultimately, students construct their own compositions using the designated essay type.

The third section of each volume provides additional research material and writing prompts to help the student. Additional facts about the topic of the book serve as a convenient source of supporting material for essays. Other features help students go beyond the book for their research. Like other Greenhaven Press books, each book in the Writing the Critical Essay series includes bibliographic listings of relevant periodical articles, books, Web sites, and organizations to contact.

Writing the Critical Essay: An Opposing Viewpoints Guide will help students master essay techniques that can be used in any discipline.

Pandemic Panic and Reality

One of the most enduring anecdotes from the 1918–1919 Spanish flu pandemic, which wiped out millions in under two years, is of four women who sat down to an evening game of bridge. By morning, three of them were dead. The funerals for these three women were by law not allowed to last more than fifteen minutes, because public gatherings even of a limited sort were considered to be dangerously infectious.

These famous victims are just three of the 50 to 100 million people who succumbed to a deadly influenza virus in eighteen months between 1918 and 1919. This horrific pandemic was sparked by a microscopic strain of flu that migrated from birds to humans. It ripped through the population so quickly that people died within days, even hours, of catching it. In less than two years, about a fifth, or 20 percent, of the world's population had become infected. The virus killed more people in twenty-five weeks than AIDS killed in twenty-five years. Or as reporter John Oxford has put it, "Let's put the 1918 influenza in perspective: it was a faster, more powerful and more efficient killer than the bubonic plague."[1] Indeed, the Spanish flu killed more people in a year and a half than the plague killed in a century, making its effect on the planet's population, health, culture, and economy significant and historic.

Today public health officials are concerned that a new strain of influenza will once again wreak havoc on people all over the planet. While several viruses are suspected by officials to be capable of becoming pandemic, chief among them is H5N1, a strain of influenza that currently afflicts birds. As of 2007, H5N1 had mutated to be able to sicken humans who were in contact with sick birds, but it was not yet transferable from human to human. However, as in the Spanish flu pandemic, officials fear that if H5N1 becomes able to be contagious within the human population, all areas of civilization—health care, transportation, the economy—would be threatened.

Few people debate that if an H5N1 pandemic were to strike, it would be anything less than devastating. The U.S. government estimates that in the event of a severe influenza pandemic, 90 million Americans, or 30 percent of the population, would get sick; 45 million would need medical care; and close to 2 million would die. The situation in the rest of the world would be even worse. Michael Osterholm, the director of the Center for Infectious Disease Research and Policy, says that an influenza pandemic would be many times more disastrous than the tsunami that struck southern Asia in 2005 and killed tens of thousands of people:

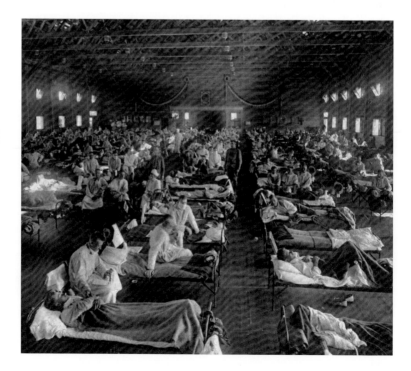

The pandemic that arose from a Spanish flu strain in 1918 killed over 40 million people. Scientists fear that a new strain of bird flu, H5N1, could result in a similar pandemic.

Duplicate it in every major urban center and rural community around the planet simultaneously, add in the paralyzing fear and panic of contagion, and we begin to get some sense of the potential of pandemic influenza. An influenza pandemic of even moderate impact will result in the biggest single human disaster ever—far greater than AIDS, 9/11, all wars in the 20th century and the recent tsunami combined. It has the potential to redirect world history as the Black Death redirected European history in the 14th century.[2]

Furthermore, the nation's transportation, health, and business industries could be expected to come to a grinding halt as quarantines froze sectors of the public and mass illness prevented the normal doing of business. According to a 2006 Harvard School of Public Health survey on pandemics, 75 percent of Americans said if a pandemic broke out, they would reduce or avoid travel, and 71 percent said they would skip public events. The economic toll this mass strike would take on all industrial sectors is incalculable.

However, while few doubt a pandemic would be devastating, many pause to question whether such an apocalyptic event is likely to occur. Several prominent voices call into question the assumption that a pandemic is imminent. Skeptics such as Peter Sandman argue that pandemics are not cyclical events, and as such cannot be overdue or called "imminent." "Flu pandemics are random," writes Sandman, "so there are no grounds to claim that a pandemic is overdue. . . . The probability of a flu pandemic hasn't increased because we've gone without one for 38 years. And if we have one this year, the probability of having another (of a different strain) the next year won't decrease."[3] The media has not helped the public put this aspect of pandemics into perspective. In fact, an increasing number of news stories have overstated the threat of many contagious diseases that failed to turn pandemic. Explains commentator Michael Fumento:

> "Hong Kong 'Bird Flu' Could be the Next Big Outbreak," blared the headlines [in 1997]. The world death toll from that "wave"? Six. And let's not forget the outbreak of SARS (severe acute respiratory syndrome) [in 2003], which led to 750 stories in the *New York Times* and *Washington Post*— one per death worldwide, as it turned out. The 71 U.S. cases of SARS, which resulted in zero deaths, did not "Overwhelm U.S. Health System," as CNN had predicted."[4]

Fumento and others argue that the panic surrounding pandemics does more harm than good. In addition to encouraging the public to consider the media and government as "crying wolf," it also focuses attentions on subjects that are minimally threatening, such as the current H5N1 bird influenza from which only a handful of people have died, and away from more devastating epidemics that have claimed millions of lives, such as AIDS. Indeed, health studies professor Peter Curson argues that

> an epidemic among birds has been used to orchestrate public panic and divert us from addressing other more pressing health issues. More than half a billion people suffer from malaria, nearly 10 million have tuberculosis, of which 2 million will die in the next year. Thirty million have died from HIV/AIDS and probably 40 million are infected. It is a great irony that we spend more time worrying about what might be, rather than what is.[5]

Whether a pandemic is imminent and how afraid of it we should be are just two of the ongoing debates surrounding this fascinating and frightening issue. Also of controversy is how many resources should be devoted to preventing a pandemic, and if one can be prevented

at all. Students will study these and other topics in the articles and essays included in *Writing the Critical Essay: An Opposing Viewpoints Guide: Pandemics*. Model essays and viewpoints expose readers to the basic arguments made about pandemics and help them develop tools to craft their own expository essays on the subject.

In 1997 the Hong Kong government warned its citizens to wear protective facial masks after a mysterious bird flu strain killed four people.

Notes

1. John Oxford, "We Can't Afford to Be Caught Napping Again," *London Times*, October 20, 2005.

2. Quoted in *Montreal Gazette*, "Bird Flu Could Kill Millions," March 9, 2005, p. A1.

3. Peter Sandman, "A Severe Pandemic Is Not Overdue— It's Not When But *If*," *CIDRAP Business Source*, February 22, 2007. www.psandman.com/CIDRAP/CIDRAP6.htm.

4. Michael Fumento, "Fuss and Feathers: Pandemic Panic over the Avian Flu," *Weekly Standard*, November 21, 2005.

5. Peter Curson, "We're Suffering a Pandemic of Panic," *Sydney Morning Herald*, January 19, 2006.

Section One:
Opposing
Viewpoints
on Pandemics

The World Is Overdue for a Pandemic

Michael Leavitt

In the following essay Michael Leavitt warns that the world is overdue for a pandemic that will kill and sicken millions. He discusses how pandemics have historically wiped out populations, crippled economies, and drastically altered culture and politics. The world has not seen such a pandemic since 1918, when a strain of flu wiped out about 40 million people. Leavitt warns that a new flu—H5N1, which bears a remarkable similarity to the 1918 strain—is being transmitted around the world. It has not yet migrated from animals to humans, but Leavitt believes it is powerful enough to do so. Leavitt urges America to put its money, time, and energy into drafting preparation plans to save as many lives as possible.

Leavitt is the secretary of Health and Human Services. He has served as head of the U.S. Environmental Protection Agency and was governor of Utah from 1992 to 2003.

Consider the following questions:

1. What effect did the A.D. 1400 pandemic have on Europe, as reported by Leavitt?
2. How many Americans would become sick and die in a modern pandemic, according to Leavitt?
3. To what extent should Americans rely on the federal government to take care of them in the event of a pandemic, according to Leavitt?

Michael Leavitt, "We're Overdue for a Pandemic," *U.S. News & World Report*, April 20, 2006. Copyright 2006 *U.S. News & World Report*, L.P. All rights reserved. Reprinted with permission.

My subject today is a difficult one to talk about. Can we just acknowledge that? Pandemics are difficult to talk about because anything you say in advance of a pandemic feels alarmist, but anything we have done once a pandemic starts seems inadequate.

So this is a function of trying to find a balance in preparing: learning to speak about this in ways that will inform but not inflame; learning to inspire communities to prepare, but not to panic.

The fact of the matter is, we—when it comes to pandemics, we are overdue, and we're underprepared. And it's necessary that we speak with candor about it and that we move with dispatch to prepare.

U.S. Health and Human Services secretary Mike Leavitt warns that no state, no matter how remote, is safe from the spread of a bird flu pandemic.

Pandemics Shape History

Pandemics are a biologic fact of life. They're part of the microbial world of viruses and bacteria and microbes that are constantly mutating, constantly adapting. They are aggressors, constantly seeking more fruitful hosts.

The history of pandemics is not so much the history of public health as it is the history of mankind, because it has been a pandemic disease that truly has—have reshaped entire nations, that have affected cultures and politics and prosperity of entire continents. As far as human history has been recorded, whether it is secular history or biblical history, the evidence of these ravaging diseases become prominent.

I go back to Athens, as far back as 400 B.C. Twenty-five percent of that great city wiped out because of a disease. We're not 100 percent sure what it was, but we know it changed the future and course of that entire region.

Roll forward periodically through every century—1400 A.D., the best-known pandemic, Black Death. Twenty-five million people on the continent of Europe died. It reshaped nations. It completely changed their culture. It affected their politics. It affected their prosperity.

A Pandemic Would Wipe Out the Population

Pandemics happen. We've had 10 pandemics in the last 300 years. In the last 100 years, we have had three pandemics: 1968, 1957—both relatively minor pandemics on a scale of pandemics. A lot of people became sick. They were highly efficient, but not many people died. They were not particularly virulent.

However, in 1918, we had what was clearly—what has to be considered clearly the world's greatest medical disaster of all time: some 40 million people across the globe perished as a result of this pandemic.

If we were to have in the United States and across the world a pandemic of similar proportion today, 90 million Americans would become ill; 45 million Americans would become sick enough that they would require some kind of serious medical attention, whether that was a clinic visit or a hospital stay. Regrettably, roughly two million people would die.

This is a very serious matter. I am not talking about a Stephen King novel here. I am talking about what happened in 1918 in this country and across the world. The fact is pandemics happen.

A Deadly Virus Is Sweeping Around the World

Now, we're concerned today because the H5N1 virus, the virus we're concerned about now, is sweeping across the world on the back of wild birds carrying this virus.

Not only are we concerned because of its broad proliferation, we're concerned because of its genetic character. Using samples that we were able to retrieve in a rather remarkable way, we've been able to use reversed genetics to identify that that virus, the 1918 virus, has great similarity to the H5N1 virus that we now see spread across the world. Should it achieve human-to-human transmissibility, which it has not in a widespread way, it would be an aggressive killer. That's why we're concerned.

So it's important that we begin to talk about it, but it's important also that we not focus entirely on this H5N1 virus because pandemics happen, and if it's not the H5N1 virus, it will be another virus at some point in the—in time, and the reality is, because they happen and because we are under prepared, we must begin to think of pandemic preparedness in its larger context, not simply the H5N1 virus. . . .

"Overdue and Underprepared"

May I suggest to you that local preparedness for the reasons that I have described is the foundation of pandemic preparedness. If there is one message on pandemic pre-

How Would a Pandemic Affect the United States?

The government estimates that millions would be sickened and killed if a pandemic were to strike in the United States.

Characteristic	Moderate	Severe
Illness	90 million (30% of the population)	90 million (30% of the population)
Outpatient medical care	45 million (50% of those ill)	45 million (50% of those ill)
Hospitalization	865,000	9,900,000
ICU care	128,750	1,485,000
Breathing apparatus needed	64,875	745,000
Deaths	209,000	1,903,000

*Estimates are based on extrapolation from past pandemics in the United States.

Taken from: www.PandemicFlu.gov.

paredness that I could leave today that you would re-member, it would be this: Any community that fails to prepare with the expectation that the federal govern-ment or for that matter the state government will be able to step forward and come to their rescue at the final hour will be tragically wrong, not because government will lack a will, not because we lack a collective wallet, but because there is no way that you can respond to every hometown in America at the same time. . . .

We don't know what a pandemic would look like, we don't know when it will come, but we do know we're overdue and underprepared. Now, that's the reason that the president has asked that we mobilize the country in preparation. I have committed to hold on his behalf 50 summits around the country. We have now accomplished 48 of those. We'll continue to the 50. There will be one in each state and some of our major cities. Over 25,000 people who are health professionals, who are school officials, who are business officials representing local and state governments, representing faith communities, have attended those, and we are now mobilizing as a nation. But we are far from prepared yet.

The president has asked the Congress for $7.1 billion. We have not had a science initiative like this, or a preparation initiative like this since the Manhattan Project[1] in this country, because we're investing substantial portions of that to invent new technologies that will provide vaccines, that will provide new antivirals, new diagnostics. We're mobilizing as a country to prepare. We're also developing check lists that will inform our collective thinking, and we're working to practice and to exercise our plans. Plans and check lists have the effect of—well, they reveal our weaknesses, but it is our weaknesses we seek, because until we know our weaknesses, we cannot improve.

Time Is Running Out to Make Preparations

A prepared nation will be a nation where every community, every business, every tribe, every community organization, every hospital, every clinic, every school,

---

A Deadly Disease Is Coming

Politicians can ignore it, and may even get away with it. But when a pandemic eventually strikes, and history suggests that one is long overdue, the consequences could be devastating. The three pandemics in the past century were all linked with a strain of bird flu that had adapted to humans. Now we have the H5N1 avian flu virus, which has already infected a number of species, including domestic poultry, pigs and humans.

Roger Highfield, "A Flu Pandemic Is Long Overdue," *London Telegraph*, February 21, 2006.

---

[1] The project to develop the first atom bomb.

every college, every day-care center, every ambulance service, every household and family has a plan.

Now, I suspect that every one of you are asking the same question I think that we all ask ourselves. Is this Y2K?[2] Is this something we're going to get all worked up over and then it won't happen? Let's hope so. There are some things we prepare for because we know they will happen. There are other things we prepare for because if they happened and we weren't prepared, they could change the nature of our society in ways that we could not respond to adequately. A pandemic is both. We need to prepare. But even if a pandemic does not happen soon, we'll be a stronger and a healthier nation because

Gravestones dating from the first week of October 1918 are just a few from the 40 million people who died of the Spanish flu pandemic.

---

[2] A computer virus that was supposed to have crippled economies at the turn of the century—but never occurred.

the pandemic preparation is the same preparation that we would make for a bioterrorism event. It's the same preparation that we would make for a medical disaster brought on by a natural consequence, like a hurricane or a tornado. It's the same kind of preparation we would make if we were to have a bioterrorism—or a nuclear event. Pandemic preparedness will make us a safer and a healthier nation. May I suggest that this is a time for real focus and one that will require our best efforts.

Analyze the essay:

1. Leavitt has held prestigious government positions for more than fifteen years. He has been a three-term governor, the head of the Environmental Protection Agency, and currently serves as the secretary of Health and Human Services at the U.S. Department of Health and Human Services. In what way do these credentials influence the weight you give his argument? Do they make you more or less inclined to agree with his position on pandemics? Explain your reasoning.

2. Leavitt argues that even if a pandemic does not strike, the United States will be a safer and healthier nation for thoroughly preparing for one. How do you think Peter Sandman, author of the following essay, would respond to this idea? Would he agree that there is no harm in preparing for a pandemic that may or may not happen? Cite evidence from the text in your answer.

The World Is Not Overdue for a Pandemic

Peter M. Sandman

In the following essay Peter M. Sandman argues it is impossible to state that the world is overdue for a pandemic. He claims that pandemics are random events that cannot be "on time" or overdue. Furthermore, he argues there is no indication that a pandemic would be debilitating. He argues the pandemics of 1957 and 1968 were mild, and claims there is every reason to expect that future ones will be, too. Finally, he disagrees that the H5N1 bird flu virus will be the cause of the next severe pandemic. While H5N1 has killed millions of birds, Sandman argues nothing indicates it will become capable of jumping from animals to humans. Sandman warns that exaggerating the pandemic risk erodes the public's trust in health organizations and creates an atmosphere of panic.

Sandman studies low-probability, high-risk issues such as pandemics and terrorism, with the goal of helping people respond rationally to frightening but low-risk situations.

Consider the following questions:

1. According to Sandman, how many pandemics might occur in the twenty-first century?
2. What do the 1957 and 1968 pandemics tell us about the severity of pandemics, according to the author?
3. What does the author mean when he suggests pandemics should be treated similarly to hurricanes?

We have no grounds for confidence that a severe pandemic is imminent. Our communications shouldn't imply otherwise.

Pandemics Are Not Cyclical—They Are Random

Medical historians tell us there have been nine influenza pandemics in the past 300 years. So one every 30 to 35 years or so, or roughly three per century, is everybody's best guess about the future frequency of influenza pandemics.

But extrapolating from nine cases is far from a sure thing. Scientists wouldn't be all that shocked if pan-

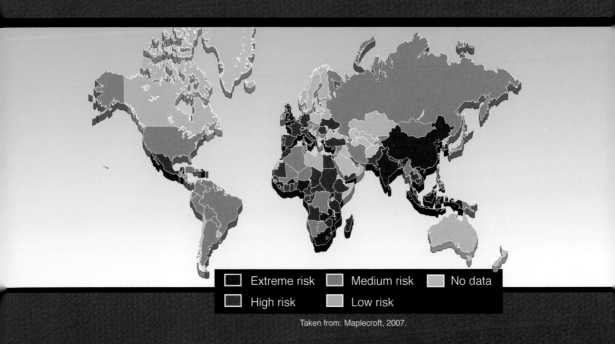

Worldwide Risk of Pandemics Is Low

According to Maplecroft, a company that determines pandemic risk around the world, the current risk of a pandemic is medium to low in most parts of the world.

Extreme risk   Medium risk   No data

High risk   Low risk

Taken from: Maplecroft, 2007.

demics started coming more frequently or less frequently. And even if the average remains three per century, it's only an average. The 21st century could still give us just one pandemic—or five.

A semi-official list of the nine pandemics since 1700, listed by the year they started is:

- 1729
- 1732
- 1781
- 1830
- 1833
- 1889
- 1918
- 1957
- 1968

There is nothing cyclic about this list. The shortest gap between pandemics is 3 years; the longest so far is 56 years. (Some authorities include 1899 and 1977 on the list as well. Adding them doesn't improve the pattern any, though it does increase the expected frequency a bit.)

Impossible to Claim a Pandemic Is Overdue

To all intents and purposes, flu pandemics are random events. So there are no grounds to claim that a pandemic is overdue simply because there hasn't been one since 1968. A random event cannot be "overdue." Risk-perception experts have a name for the mistaken view that random events are patterned. They call it the gambler's fallacy—named for the tendency of many roulette players to imagine that a number is overdue because it hasn't come up all night. (The other gambler's fallacy is imagining that a different number is "hot" because it has come up several times in quick succession.)

Bottom line: The probability of a flu pandemic hasn't increased because we've gone without one for 38 years.

And if we have one this year, the probability of having another (of a different strain) the next year won't decrease.

"Not When but If"

Still, scientists would be pretty surprised if influenza pandemics simply stopped happening altogether. So it's fair to say about the next flu pandemic that "it's not if, but when." And a lot of people have said just that. A Google search for "pandemic" plus "not if but when" yielded about 1,000 links (some of them from CIDRAP).

But this is not a fair thing to say about a severe flu pandemic. By most accounts, 1918 was the mother of all flu pandemics, worse than any (or nearly any) we know about before or since. Most survivors of the 1918 pandemic remembered losing friends or relatives to it. By contrast, most of us who lived through the pandemics of 1957 and 1968 barely noticed.

Maybe a pandemic as bad as 1918 happens once every 300 years or so. (There was apparently a big one in 1580, too.) Maybe 1957 and 1968 will turn out to be the exceptions, and most future pandemics will be more like 1918. We don't know. That's why I say that, when we're talking about a severe pandemic, something as bad as 1918 or worse, it's not when but if.

Precisely because 1957 and 1968 were so forgettable, the claim that future pandemics are inevitable is often heard as a claim that severe pandemics are inevitable. And that's just not true.

The Problem with Crying "Pandemic"

Every year we get told the new plague is about to arrive. A few years ago it was hantavirus, then Ebola, then West Nile virus, then SARS. And every year it doesn't. Infectious-disease experts have learned that they can get attention for their cause by talking about exotic new diseases, not things like hand washing or wound sterility. I'm very concerned that by crying wolf, they're in danger of losing credibility and getting resources put into the wrong things. [Tuberculosis], malaria, and HIV aren't sexy new diseases, but each year they kill millions of people. To the best of our knowledge, influenza pandemics are rare, random events. You're never "overdue" for a random event.

Richard Schabas quoted in David Stipp, "Is the Risk Overblown? Calling a Pandemic 'Overdue' Is a Misnomer Worthy of Chicken Little," *Fortune Magazine*, March 7, 2005.

Past Pandemics Cannot Tell Us About Future Ones

Or it may be heard as a claim that the influenza strain that currently dominates news coverage, H5N1, will inevitably launch a pandemic. That's not true either. H5N1 has been around at least since 1997 without becoming capable of efficient human-to-human transmission. Does that mean that it probably won't? We don't know. H5N1 has proved incredibly deadly to both poultry (millions) and people (scores). Does that mean that if it becomes capable of efficient human-to-human transmission, the pandemic it launches will be a severe one? We don't know that either.

Government health organizations may actually run a risk of panic worldwide by overdoing pandemic drills, thus, losing the public's trust if a pandemic does not occur.

Because pandemics are random occurrences, taking precautions, such as wearing facial masks, may be unnecessary.

Right now is the first time we've ever been able to watch closely as a new bird flu strain either does or doesn't lead to a human pandemic. So we can't say whether H5N1 is acting like past bird flus that later launched bad pandemics, or past bird flus that later launched mild pandemics, or past bird flus that never launched pandemics at all.

In recent months there have been a few news stories on the theme: "Whatever became of the bird flu scare?

How come the predicted pandemic didn't happen?" What's missing from these very damaging stories is the crucial fact that the pandemic risk hasn't abated simply because no pandemic has materialized so far.

Pandemic preparedness advocates blame these sorts of stories on the short attention span of the media. But we who give the mainstream media their information—including CIDRAP—deserve some of the blame ourselves. If reporters and the public earlier got the impression that a severe H5N1 pandemic was imminent, they got it from us. The misimpression that the risk was necessarily imminent and the misimpression that the risk is now past are identical twins. The first gave rise to the second.

Overstating the Danger of Pandemics Erodes Trust

Two closely connected risk-communication principles are at stake here.

The first principle is to acknowledge uncertainty. An overconfident risk communicator is likely to generate skepticism in the audience even before the truth is known. And if the truth turns out to be different from your confident prediction, trust in you erodes. That doesn't mean you shouldn't make predictions. It means your predictions shouldn't sound more confident than the facts justify. Talk about H5N1 the way weather forecasters talk about a distant hurricane. It might be headed our way—or not. It might strengthen—or weaken. We need to track it closely, stockpile essential supplies, and make contingency plans. Will it be category 5 or category 2? Will it hit here or go elsewhere? It's not when, but *if*.

The second principle deals specifically with worst-case scenarios—that is, low-probability, high-magnitude risks. The wisdom of taking precautions depends not just on the probability of a risk, but also on its magnitude. When a risk is awful enough, precautions make sense, even though the risk may be unlikely and the precautions may be wasted. We don't buy fire insurance because we're confident our house will catch fire; we buy it because a fire could be devastating. And wise insurance salespeople don't tell us that we're overdue for a fire. They don't claim that it's not if but when our house will burn.

Analyze the essay:

1. Sandman closes his essay by likening health officials to insurance salespeople. What point is he trying to make? How does it support his argument?

2. In this essay Sandman uses history, facts, and examples to make his argument that the world is not overdue for a pandemic. He does not, however, use any quotations to support his point. If you were to rewrite this article and insert quotations, what authorities might you quote from? Where would you place these quotations to bolster the points Sandman makes?

A Bird Flu Pandemic Is Likely to Occur

Pat Jackson Allen

In the following viewpoint Pat Jackson Allen argues that humans are dangerously at risk for a bird flu pandemic. She explains that a strain of bird flu, H1N1, caused the 1918 Spanish flu pandemic that killed millions of people. Today a new strain of bird flu, H5N1, similarly threatens human health. She explains that for the time being, H5N1 has been contained to the avian population. But the flu is expected to jump to humans due to the contact farmers have with their livestock's blood, saliva, and other excretions. Allen explains that when this transference occurs, the human population will be at risk because it has no natural defense against this strain of flu. Allen expects that just a moderate bird flu outbreak could kill a quarter of the U.S. population and cost billions in medical care and economic loss. For these reasons Allen recommends all nations to prevent a bird flu pandemic while there is still time.

Allen is a professor at the Yale School of Nursing.

Consider the following questions:

1. According to the author, why is H1N1, the flu strain that caused the great pandemic of 1918, no longer a threat to human health?
2. What does the phrase "antigenic shift" mean in the context of the viewpoint?
3. Why are authorities concerned that early signs that H5N1 has mutated from birds to humans will go undetected?

Pat Jackson Allen, "Avian Influenza Pandemic: Not If, But When," *Pediatric Nursing*, vol. 32, April 10, 2006, pp. 76–81. Copyright © 2006 Jannetti Publications, Inc. Reproduced by permission.

Dire predictions of a "Bird Flu" pandemic have been reported in multiple public media sources. The director of the Centers for Disease Control and Prevention (CDC) labeled avian influenza as "the most important threat that we are facing now" and a United Nations (U.N.) top health official stated "the range of deaths could be anything between 5 and 150 million." President Bush has held White House strategy meetings with health officials and vaccine and antiviral drug developers trying to increase development and production of drugs for possible use in a pandemic. The Bush administration released the National Strategy for Pandemic Influenza report in early November, 2005 outlining regional, state, and federal responsibilities for containment and treatment during a pandemic. The Senate voted in late September 2005 to provide the CDC $4 billion dollars to stockpile antiviral medication in preparation for a possible influenza pandemic, and in November the Bush administration asked for an additional $7.1 billion for vaccine development, additional antiviral medication, and development of emergency plans. The President reported that advisors were evaluating the use of the military to enforce a mass quarantine if a serious pandemic occurs, something that has not been done in this country in over 125 years, though public health officials were quick to reassure the public that this would likely not be necessary.

So, what is "Bird Flu" or avian influenza, and why are public health officials so concerned?

Understanding Bird Flu

All influenza A viruses originate in birds, and wild birds are the natural host for influenza. Most subtypes of influenza A do not cause illness and death in birds but may cause morbidity and mortality if transferred to other mammals, including humans. An influenza A viral subtype (H1N1) from birds is now thought to have caused the great influenza pandemic of 1918, known as the "Spanish flu," that killed over 675,000 people in the

United States and an estimated 50 million people world-wide. This extraordinary virus "killed more people in a year than the Black Death of the Middle Ages killed in a century; it killed more people in twenty-four weeks than AIDS has killed in twenty-four years." The H1N1 influenza A virus circulates in the human population today but it has mutated into a much less lethal form, and much of the population has developed antibodies against this virus reducing the number of people infected and able to spread the virus. . . .

The current H5N1 avian influenza A is a highly pathogenic virus having killed over a 100 million birds in

Millions of birds suspected to be infected with the flu strain H5N1 have been slaughtered to prevent further outbreaks.

2003 and 2004 in Vietnam, Cambodia, Laos, China, Japan, Indonesia, South Korea, and Thailand, either from disease or attempts by governments to stop the spread of the virus by culling millions of domestic birds and poultry. . . .

The H5N1 virus in birds has extended into Europe and northern China by the normal migration patterns of wild birds and now threatens to spread to Africa. Wild birds come in contact with domestic birds and poultry raised by small farmers and spread the H5N1 virus through their saliva, excretions, and blood. Families throughout Asia and Africa raise poultry for food and often live in very close contact with their poultry and livestock. Many of these family farms are far from health facilities or supervision by agricultural officials. For this reason, world health authorities are concerned that early indications of a change in the virus allowing for easy transmission of H5N1 virus to people or human-to-human transmission, will not be identified quickly and containment established before wide-spread illness occurs.

Humans Are Vulnerable to New Strains of Bird Flu

Changes in influenza viruses occur all the time. The influenza vaccine administered each year in the United States has to be changed to reflect this antigenic drift. The current vaccine has two influenza A viruses, H1N1 and H3N2, now common in humans but previously avian viruses, and an influenza B virus, which is strictly a human virus. WHO [World Health Organization] is closely monitoring the antigenic and genetic evolution of the circulating H5N1 virus and has identified changes in the virus during the past year and since it first infected people in 1997. So far the changes have been small, but there is growing concern that a major change called "antigenic shift" will occur in the virus structure creating a new virus more easily transmitted to humans.

One mechanism of antigenic shift can occur through the process of "reassortment." Reassortment occurs when a mammal is infected with two types of virus, for example, if a person were to contract both the H5N1 virus and the H1N1 virus during the usual influenza season for humans. These two circulating viruses could exchange, or reassort, segments of their genetic structure producing a new viral strain that could be easily communicated from person-to-person. The winter human influenza season, the wide-spread distribution of H5N1 in birds, and its recent discovery in other mammals including the pig, all increase the likelihood of reassortment occurring in the near future. If the reassortment results in a virus that is transmitted from person-to-person, a pandemic will occur

Bird Flu Around the World

As of 2007 the bird flu strain H5N1 had spread from Asia to Europe, killing both humans and birds.

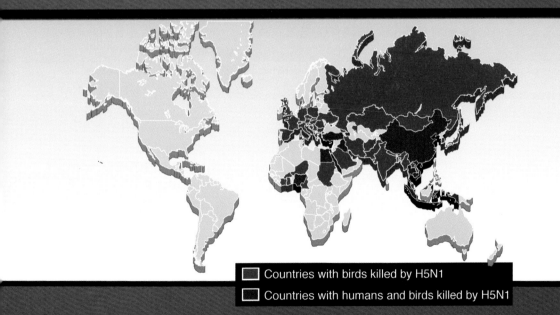

Countries with birds killed by H5N1
Countries with humans and birds killed by H5N1

Taken from: www.wikipedia.com.

because humans do not have an "antigenic history" with H5NI HPAI. If the reassorted virus maintains its virulence, millions world-wide could die.

Pandemics occur on average 3 times a century, and the last pandemic due to influenza A was over 50 years ago. The 20th century had three influenza pandemics: the 1918 "Spanish flu" previously mentioned; and two less lethal pandemics, the 1957–1958 "Asian flu," an H2N2 virus that killed 70,000 people in the United States; and the 1968–1969 "Hong Kong flu," an H3N2 influenza A virus that killed 34,000 people in the U.S. and resulted in world-wide health and economic disruption. The last two pandemics resulted in deaths primarily in the traditional at-risk groups, the elderly, and infirmed; but the 1918 pandemic and the current H5N1 infections have shown a higher mortality in the otherwise healthy young child and young adult.

The Experts Agree the Threat Is Severe

There are perhaps 5,000 influenza virologists worldwide and I personally know of only two who think the risk from the new avian flu, H5N1, has been exaggerated. We want to do everything to stop an outbreak by pinpointing its source, calculating the critical infectiousness of the virus and deluging people in the affected area with antiviral drugs and vaccines.

John Oxford, "We Can't Afford to Be Caught Napping Again," *London Times*, October 20, 2005.

A Bird Flu Pandemic Would Be Devastating

The World Health Organization has labeled the current H5N1 situation a "Phase 3 Pandemic Alert" (human infection with a new subtype has occurred but no, or limited, human-to-human spread). Phase 4 of the Pandemic Alert would involve small clusters of human-to-human transmission with only localized spread and the hope of containment, while Phase 5 would involve larger clusters of human infections and the scientific belief that the virus is more compatible to human transmission. Phase 6 is the pandemic phase with sustained transmission in the general population.

Although the world is better prepared today to monitor and attempt to control a new pandemic, the lack of a recent viral pandemic similar to the H5N1 influenza A virus means that the world population has little to no preexisting natural immunity to protect against this serious illness. A pandemic of even moderate severity is estimated to affect a quarter of the U.S. population (67 million), with almost 550,000 deaths, and 2,358,000 hospitalizations. The health care costs in the United States alone have been estimated to be $181 billion for a moderate pandemic, with the World Bank estimating the loss of $800 billion in gross domestic production world-wide if a pandemic strikes. Even industrialized countries like the United States would be overwhelmed by the burden on the health care system, lack of adequate intensive care facilities, respirators, medications, medical supplies, and healthy health professionals able to provide care. A pandemic, by definition, affects the whole world, and consequently all nations would be affected, and the usual effort by developed countries to assist less developed countries in time of disaster may not be possible or a political priority. . . .

We Must Act While There Is Still Time

The world is better prepared today to monitor and isolate a new influenza virus than it has ever been before. But the potential spread of infection from continent to continent is easier today than ever before due to our global economy and ease of travel. Developing countries will bear an increased burden of illness and death with a new influenza pandemic, as they have with other infectious diseases such as malaria, tuberculosis, and HIV-AIDS, and with limited availability of medications and health care resources, it is unclear whether or not developed countries will be willing or able to provide the necessary assistance to attempt to contain a new virus.

Nurses, especially pediatric nurses, will be many of the first responders to a pandemic and must be knowledgeable about this impending pandemic and the symptoms, treatment, and prevention measures needed

Birds and their cages are burned in a neighborhood in Indonesia where residents in the area reportedly died of bird flu.

to limit morbidity and mortality among our vulnerable pediatric and young adult population. If the world is fortunate, H5N1 will not easily spread between humans for a few more years, giving the scientific community time to develop and perfect an effective vaccine. If the world unites to identify, contain, and treat an outbreak in the next year, we may be able to stop a deadly pandemic at its source. Health professionals from WHO and CDC believe the question is not "are we going to have another avian influenza pandemic," but "when will it occur and will the world be ready."

Analyze the essay:

1. Allen states that pandemics occur on average three times per century, and because the last pandemic was more than fifty years ago, the world is overdue for one. How do you think each of the other authors in this section might respond to this statement? List each author and write two to three sentences on what you think their response might be.

2. Allen discusses the deaths that have occurred in the bird flu population from H5N1 and argues that this strain of flu will cause millions of deaths in the human population. What assumption must she make in order for her argument to make sense? Isolate the assumption. Then, using evidence from the texts you have read, discuss whether you think this assumption can reasonably be made.

A Bird Flu Pandemic Is Not Likely to Occur

Michael Fumento

In the following essay Michael Fumento argues that Americans should not worry that a bird flu pandemic is about to strike. He says there is no reason to suspect that H5N1 will mutate from birds to humans—and even if it did, it might take millions of years to do so. He cites studies of similar flu strains that have shown that even if a strain of H5N1 adapted to humans, it is not likely to be passed easily from human to human, which would be necessary to cause a pandemic. Fumento believes that a bird flu pandemic is a myth that helps government health agencies increase their budgets. He scolds organizations for profiting from fear and concludes that those who have panicked about a bird flu pandemic have done more damage than bird flu itself.

Fumento has written several articles on the bird flu controversy. They have appeared in the *Weekly Standard*, where this essay was originally published.

Consider the following questions:

1. How many new cases of bird flu were identified in 2006? What explanation does Fumento offer for the increase?
2. What does Fumento say is the true death rate from H5N1?
3. What do H5N1 injections from 1998 show about the strain's ability to mutate, as reported by Fumento?

Michael Fumento, "The Chicken Littles Were Wrong," *Weekly Standard*, vol. 12, December 25, 2006. © Copyright 2007, News Corporation, Weekly Standard. All rights reserved. Reproduced by permission.

It's that time of year again—avian flu panic season. As the weather turns colder in the northern hemisphere and the flu starts making its annual rounds, the media and their anointed health experts are chirping and squawking once again about how we could be blindsided by a pandemic that some have estimated could kill a billion persons worldwide. New books like *The Coming Avian Flu Pandemic* join last year's *The Monster at Our Door: The Global Threat of Avian Flu*. . . .

Profiting from Panic

Not coincidentally, an avian flu bureaucracy has become entrenched. Like all bureaucracies, it will fight to survive

The bird flu strain H5N1, magnified in gold, has killed a few people, but has not yet mutated and thus currently poses no threat to large numbers of people.

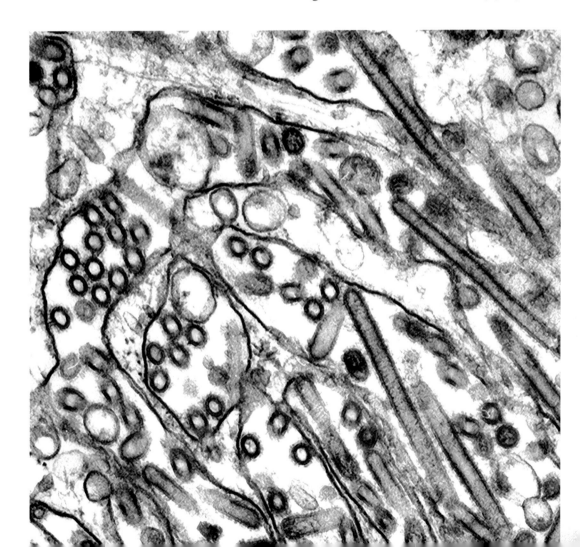

and thrive, egging on governments to provide ever more money. The alarmingly titled *2006 Guide to Surviving Bird Flu* is published by no less than the Department of Health and Human Services. Never mind that no one in this country has yet even contracted bird flu. Congress last year allocated $3.8 billion to prevent the ballyhooed catastrophe (Bush requested almost twice) that amount). The latest "scary news," promulgated in the November 23 [2006] issue of the *New England Journal of Medicine* by über-alarmist Robert Webster of St. Jude Memorial Children's Hospital, is that human cases of H5N1 contracted from birds are continuing to increase. Indeed, confirmed cases for 2006 are running ahead of those for last year. But the difference is slight; 97 worldwide for all of last year versus 111 through the end of November 2006. This difference could be entirely explained by better surveillance. Moreover, the real concern is not sporadic bird-to-human transmission, but human-to-human transmission. Far more people die of tuberculosis in an hour than all those known to have died from H5N1.

So it's time to revisit the allegations and show that as small as the risk was a year ago, it's nevertheless dropped considerably since.

A Bird Flu Pandemic Is Unlikely to Occur

A flu pandemic can come about in two ways. One way is for the virus to randomly mutate to become easily transmissible between humans. "Randomly" is the key word here. There are no evolutionary pressures to make H5N1 adapt better to humans. Given enough time, H5N1 might mutate so that it could under the right conditions become pandemic. But that could take millions of years, during which time it would be more likely to mutate itself out of existence. H5N1 was first identified in Scottish chickens in 1959. It has been flying around the globe for close to half a century and hasn't done a number on us yet. There's absolutely no reason to think it will pick this year or next to do so.

A Time Line of Modern Bird Flu

Confirmed instances of avian influenza viruses infecting humans since 1997 include:

1997

H5N1, Hong Kong 1997: Eighteen people were hospitalized and six died from H5N1 acquired from contact with sick poultry. To control the outbreak, authorities killed about 1.5 million chickens to remove the source of the virus. This was the first time an avian influenza A virus transmission directly from birds to humans had been found.

H9N2, China and Hong Kong, 1999: Several human infections with H9N2 avian influenza were identified. Evidence suggested that poultry was the source of infection and the main mode of transmission was from bird to human.

H7N2, Virginia, 2002: One person was found to have serologic evidence of infection with H7N2 after an outbreak among poultry in the Shenandoah Valley poultry production area.

H5N1, China and Hong Kong, 2003: Three members of a Hong Kong family traveled to China and contracted serious infections from an unknown source. Two were confirmed to have H5N1 infections. Two died and one survived.

H7N7, Netherlands, 2003: Multiple outbreaks of H7N7 occurred on farms, infecting poultry, pigs, and humans. Eighty-nine people were confirmed to have H7N7 influenza infection, seventy eight with conjunctivitis; five cases of conjunctivitis and influenza-like illness with cough, fever, and muscle aches; two cases of influenza-like illness only; four "other symptoms"; and one death in a veterinarian who developed acute respiratory distress syndrome after visiting one of the affected farms.

H9N2, Hong Kong, 2003: Low pathogenic avian influenza A (H9N2) infection was confirmed in a child in Hong Kong. The child was hospitalized and recovered.

H7N2, New York, 2003: An adult with serious underlying medical conditions was admitted to a hospital in New York with respiratory symptoms. Subsequent confirmatory tests conducted in March 2004 showed that the patient had been infected with avian influenza A (H7N2) virus.

H7N3, Canada, 2004: In February 2004 human infections of highly pathogenic avian influenza A (H7N3) among poultry workers were associated with an H7N3 outbreak among poultry.

H5N1, Thailand and Vietnam, 2004: Between December 30, 2003, and March 17, 2004, thirty-five cases with twenty-three deaths of confirmed H5N1 were reported in Thailand and Vietnam.

H5N1, Cambodia, China, Indonesia, Thailand, and Vietnam, 2005: Multiple human H5N1 infections occurred. At least two persons in Vietnam were thought to have been infected with H5N1 through consumption of uncooked duck blood.

H5N1, Azerbaijan, Cambodia, China, Djibouti, Egypt, Indonesia, Iraq, Thailand, and Turkey, 2006: Multiple human H5N1 infections occurred. While most of these occurred as a result of contact with infected poultry, in Azerbaijan, the most plausible cause of exposure to H5N1 in several instances of human infection is thought to be contact with infected dead wild birds (swans).

Present

Another scenario is that somebody with human flu could contract avian flu at the same time and the two flus could "reassort" into hybrid avian-human flu. The last two flu epidemics in the 20th century—1957–58 and 1968–69—were caused by such hybrids. We can help this possibility by vaccinating as many people as possible (especially Southeast Asian poultry farmers) against human flu, thus reducing the potential number of "mixing vessels." Programs underway to keep farmers away from poultry droppings and spittle (birds don't sneeze or cough) will also help.

Ferreting Out the Truth

A fascinating study in the August 8, 2006, issue of *Proceedings of the National Academy of Sciences* would seem to indicate we're already pretty safe from a human-avian hybrid. Researchers from the U.S. Centers for Disease

© 2006 Wright, *The Detroit News*, and Politicalcartoons.com.

Control and Prevention conducted three separate studies with ferrets, which are among the few animals known to suffer from and transmit human flu. The ferrets were infected with several H5N1 strains in addition to a common human influenza virus (H3N2) that circulates almost every year. The infected animals were then either placed in the same cage with uninfected ferrets to test transmissibility by close contact or in adjacent cages with perforated walls to test spread of the virus from respiratory droplets.

The research showed that the H3N2 virus passed easily by droplets (ferrets do sneeze and do not use handkerchiefs) but the H5N1 virus did not spread—the same thing we're seeing in humans infected with H5N1 from birds. . . .

Other researchers have found the explanation for a phenomenon that was already clear but unexplained—that H5N1 virtually never spreads from human to human and, if it does, it's only after prolonged contact. This contrasts with human flu, which can be contracted via a single cough or sneeze. A *Nature* magazine study published last March [2006] found that while avian flu can infect human lungs, it cannot infect most of the cells lining the nose, throat, and sinuses. Moreover, it tends not to penetrate deeply into the lungs. "It has been an enigma why people get sick and die from H5N1 avian flu virus, but the virus does not spread well in humans," study leader and University of Wisconsin virologist Yoshihiro Kawaoka told WebMD. "Our finding explains it."

Death Rates from Bird Flu Have Been Exaggerated

Ersatz experts like Laurie Garrett, a renowned pandemic panic-monger, warn of a horrific mortality rate from the bird flu virus. "Right now in human beings, it kills 55 percent of the people it infects," she told ABC News's *Primetime* last year [2006]. St. Jude's alarmist Webster

Critics believe that the bird flu pandemic has been exaggerated by government health agencies in order to increase their budgets.

referred to a similar death rate in his *New England Journal of Medicine* article, and the media routinely parrot it. By comparison, the devastating 1918–1919 Spanish flu is believed to have killed 2.5 percent to 5 percent of those it infected. The death rate in a typical flu season is less than 1 percent. It's true that, of bird flu cases recorded by the World Health Organization, 59 percent have died. But this is a mere artifact with an obvious

explanation: Only people with the most severe cases go to the hospital and become part of the dataset.

As to what the true mortality rate is, over a three-month period in 2004, Swedish and Vietnamese researchers studied 45,478 residents in a rural district in Vietnam that had H5N1 outbreaks to find out how many had contact with sick birds and how many had flu-like illnesses. They published their results in January 2006 in the *Archives of Internal Medicine*. They found that of 8,149 who had a flu-like illness, 650 to 750 probably caught it from birds. Yet for all of 2004, the World Health Organization data indicated only 29 Vietnamese cases with 20 deaths. Thus what might seem to be a horrific mortality rate of almost two in three, or 69 percent, appears to be actually around one in 140 or 0.71 percent. This, in the rural portion of a Communist country with a state-run medical system. That 0.71 percent is in the same range as seasonal human flu.

> ## A Pandemic of Panic
>
> The media coverage and the political reaction makes bird flu appear far more widespread, contagious and threatening than the reality. Endless TV shots of public health staff in bio-hazard suits destroying thousands of chickens have incited unwarranted public anxiety. . . . [Meanwhile] more than half a billion people suffer from malaria, nearly 10 million have tuberculosis, of which 2 million will die in the next year. Thirty million have died from HIV/AIDS and probably 40 million are infected. It is a great irony that we spend more time worrying about what might be, rather than what is.
>
> Peter Curson, "We're Suffering a Pandemic of Panic," *Sydney Morning Herald*, January 19, 2006.

More good news from Vietnam, incidentally, is that it has reported zero cases in 2006. Why? As I wrote last year [2005], "Vietnam appears to be making a heroic effort to inoculate all of its poultry." If you can keep poultry from getting flu, you've knocked down the chance of a human pandemic from close to zero to absolute zero. . . .

Vaccines Can Help Reduce the Risk

It's common to hear stockpiling vaccines is futile since it's impossible to say what the effectiveness of a vaccine based on the virus presently in humans exposed to birds will be when it's altered to a point where it's going from human to human. But there was already evidence last year [2005] that such a mutation shouldn't be a problem. Scientists tested blood from people who had received an experimental vaccine against a 1997 strain of H5N1 and found it provoked a powerful cross-reaction from a strain that killed several Vietnamese in 2004.

Newer research by Dr. John Treanor and colleagues at the University of Rochester, presented on October 13 [2006] at a meeting of the Infectious Diseases Society of America supports these findings. Treanor's team studied people who'd been vaccinated against the Hong Kong strain of the H5N1 virus in 1998. Each was vaccinated again this year [2006] with a booster shot to fight the strain found in Vietnam. A second test group received only shots for the Vietnam strain in 2005. Those who received shots back in 1998 developed better protection than those with just the 2005 vaccination. Thus for all the talk about how rapidly H5N1 mutates, injections from 1998 were still protective. On the other hand, a seasonal human flu injection from 1998 would be worthless.

Hysteria Over Bird Flu Is Unwarranted and Dangerous

This is both evidence that H5N1 is not mutating like gangbusters and that we can quite possibly amass enough vaccine to protect every reachable person on the planet without having to build a new stockpile each year. Hysteria over an avian flu pandemic has been very good for the Chicken Little media, authors, ambitious health officials, drug companies, and even Bush bashers. (An alarmist fantasy published by *Nature* magazine in May 2005 concluded by predicting a pandemic outbreak in December of last year [2005], laying the blame entirely at the president's feet.) But even as many of the panic-mongers have begun to lie low, the vestiges of hysteria remain—as do the misallocations of billions of dollars from more serious health problems. Too bad no one ever holds the doomsayers accountable for the damage they've done.

Analyze the essay:

1. Fumento characterizes his opponents as "über-alarmists" and "panic-mongers." In your opinion, do such characterizations strengthen or weaken his argument? Did they make his ideas more interesting to read, or did you feel they detracted from his points? Explain your reasoning.

2. Both Michael Fumento and Pat Jackson Allen, author of the previous essay, discuss "reassortment" in their essays. Recount how each author explains what reassortment is and what effect it could have on a bird flu pandemic. What similarities exist in their explanations? What differences? After reading both essays, how likely do you think it is that a severe bird flu pandemic will occur?

A Multipronged Approach Is Required to Prevent a Pandemic

Michael T. Osterholm

In the following essay Michael T. Osterholm explains that a multipronged effort is required to prepare for the next pandemic. He argues a pandemic is likely to occur, though no one can say when. He recommends that world leaders research how influenza viruses operate, and develop an effective flu vaccine. Plans need to be drafted for how vaccines would be stockpiled and distributed. Hospitals and emergency facilities must be readied to prepare for the influx of thousands, even millions, of people who need medical care, he argues. Finally, he recommends that schools, companies, and organizations make personalized plans for how to deal with a pandemic. Osterholm warns that the next pandemic could be the deadliest history has ever seen, and humanity must be prepared to deal with it.

Osterholm is the director of the Center for Infectious Disease Research and Policy and a professor of public health at the University of Minnesota, Minneapolis.

Consider the following questions:

1. What change does Osterholm recommend making to the egg-based manufacturing process for vaccines, and why?
2. What would be the result of a travel ban due to a pandemic outbreak, according to Osterholm?
3. What is ARDS, and how many deaths (U.S. and worldwide) does Osterholm say it might cause if a new pandemic were to hit?

Michael T. Osterholm, "Preparing for the Next Pandemic," *New England Journal of Medicine*, vol. 352, May 5, 2005, pp. 1839–1842. Copyright © 2005 Massachusetts Medical Society. All rights reserved. Reproduced by permission.

Annual influenza epidemics are like Minnesota winters—all are challenges, but some are worse than others. No matter how well we prepare, some blizzards take quite a toll. Each year, despite our efforts to increase the rates of influenza vaccination in our most vulnerable populations, unpredictable factors largely determine the burden of influenza disease and related deaths. During a typical year in the United States, 30,000 to 50,000 persons die as a result of influenzavirus infection, and the global death toll is about 20 to 30 times as high as the toll in this country. We usually accept this outcome as part of the cycle of life. Only when a vaccine shortage occurs or young children die suddenly does the public demand that someone step forward to change the course of the epidemic. Unfortunately, the fragile and limited production capacity of our 1950s egg-based technology for producing influenza vaccine and the lack of a national commitment to universal annual influenza vaccination mean that influenza epidemics will continue to present a substantial public health challenge for the foreseeable future.

An influenza pandemic has always been a great global infectious-disease threat. There have been 10 pandemics of influenza A in the past 300 years. A recent analysis showed that the pandemic of 1918 and 1919 killed 50 million to 100 million people,[1] and although its severity is often considered anomalous, the pandemic of 1830 through 1832 was similarly severe—it simply occurred when the world's population was smaller. Today, with a world population of 6.5 billion—more than three times that in 1918—even a relatively "mild" pandemic could kill many millions of people.

Influenza experts recognize the inevitability of another pandemic. When will it begin? Will it be caused by H5N1, the avian influenzavirus strain currently circulating in Asia? Will its effect rival that of 1918 or be more muted, as was the case in the pandemics of 1957 and 1968? Nobody knows.

So how can we prepare? One key step is to rapidly ramp up research related to the production of an effective vaccine, as the Department of Health and Human Services is doing. In addition to clinical research on the immunogenicity of influenza vaccines, urgent needs include basic research on the ecology and biology of influenzaviruses, studies of the epidemiologic role of various animal and bird species, and work on early interventions and risk assessment.[2] Equally urgent is the development of cell-culture technology for production of vaccine that can replace our egg-based manufacturing process. Today, making the 300 million doses of influenza vaccine needed annually worldwide requires more than 350 million chicken eggs and six or more months; a cell-culture approach may produce much higher antigen yields and be faster. After such a process was developed, we would also need assured industrial capacity to produce sufficient vaccine for the world's population during the earliest days of an emerging pandemic.

Beyond research and development, we need a public health approach that includes far more than drafting of general plans, as several countries and states have done. We need a detailed operational blueprint of the best way to get through 12 to 24 months of a pandemic.

What if the next pandemic were to start tonight? If it were determined that several cities in Vietnam had major outbreaks of H5N1 infection associated with high mortality, there would be a scramble to stop the virus from entering other countries by greatly reducing or even prohibiting foreign travel and trade. The global economy would come to a halt, and since we could not expect appropriate vaccines to be available for many months and we have very limited stockpiles of antiviral drugs, we would be facing a 1918-like scenario.

Production of a vaccine would take a minimum of six months after isolation of the circulating strain, and given the capacity of all the current international vaccine manufacturers, supplies during those next six months would be limited to fewer than a billion monovalent doses. Since two doses may be required for protection, we could vaccinate fewer than 500 million people—approximately 14 percent of the world's population. And owing to our global "just-in-time delivery" economy, we would have no surge capacity for health care, food supplies, and many other products and services. For example, in the

People wait in line for flu shots. Many believe that a bird flu epidemic could be fought with similar measures.

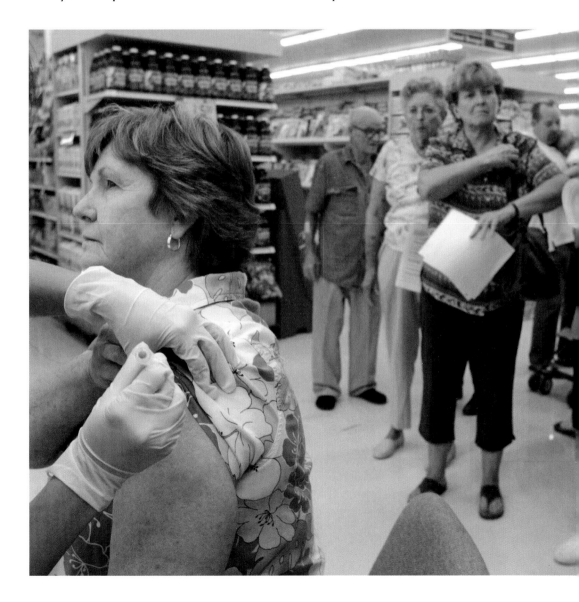

United States today, we have only 105,000 mechanical ventilators, 75,000 to 80,000 of which are in use at any given time for everyday medical care; during a garden-variety influenza season, more than 100,000 are required. In a pandemic, most patients with influenza who needed ventilation would not have access to it.

We have no detailed plans for staffing the temporary hospitals that would have to be set up in high-school gymnasiums and community centers—and that might need to remain in operation for one or two years. Health care workers would become ill and die at rates similar to, or even higher than, those in the general public. Judging by our experience with the severe acute respiratory syndrome (SARS), some health care workers would not show up for duty. How would communities train and use volunteers? If the pandemic wave were spreading slowly enough, could immune survivors of an early wave, particularly health care workers, become the primary response corps?

Health care delivery systems and managed-care organizations have done little planning for such a scenario. Who, for instance, would receive the extremely limited antiviral agents that will be available? We need to develop a national, and even an international, consensus on the priorities for the use of antiviral drugs well before the pandemic begins. In addition, we have no way of urgently increasing production of critical items such as antiviral drugs, masks for respiratory protection, or antibiotics for the treatment of secondary bacterial infections. Even under today's relatively stable operating conditions, eight different antiinfective agents are in short supply because of manufacturing problems. Nor do we have detailed plans for handling the massive number of dead bodies that would soon exceed our ability to cope with them.

What if an H5N1 influenza pandemic began not now but a year from now? We would still need to plan with fervor for local nonmedical as well as medical prepared-

Pandemic Influenza: How It Starts

Influenza viruses constantly change and produce new strains. A pandemic starts if a new influenza virus emerges. In order to become a pandemic virus, an animal virus, usually an avian (bird) virus must mutate or mix with a human influenza virus and become able to spread from person to person. A pandemic influenza virus can spread quickly because it is new and most people have no immunity. A vaccine can be researched and made only after the new virus is identified. Antiviral treatment or drugs may be available during a pandemic, but they may be in limited supply, and their effectiveness against the pandemic strain is not yet known.

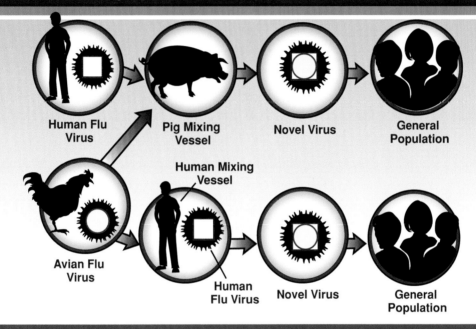

Taken from: National Health Services, England.

ness. Planning for a pandemic must be on the agenda of every public health agency, school board, manufacturing plant, investment firm, mortuary, state legislature, and food distributor. Health professionals must become much more proficient in "risk communication," so that they can effectively provide the facts—and acknowledge the unknowns—to a frightened population.[3]

With another year of lead time, vaccine might have a more central role in our response. Although the manufacturing capacity would still be limited, strategies such as developing antigen-sparing formulations—that is, intradermal formulations that take advantage of copious numbers of dendritic cells for antigen processing or formulations including adjuvants to boost the immune response—might extend the vaccine supply. Urgent planning efforts are required to ensure that we have the syringes and other essential equipment, as well as the workforce, for effective delivery. Finally, a detailed plan for vaccine allocation will be needed—before the crisis, not during it.

What if the pandemic were 10 years away and we embarked today on a worldwide influenza Manhattan Project aimed at producing and delivering a pandemic vaccine for everyone in the world soon after the onset of sustained human-to-human transmission? In this scenario, we just might make a real difference.

The current system of producing and distributing influenza vaccine is broken, both technically and financially. The belief that we can greatly advance manufacturing technology and expand capacity in the normal course of increasing our annual vaccination coverage is flawed. At our current pace, it will take generations for meaningful advances to be made. Our goal should be to develop a new cell-culture-based vaccine that includes antigens that are present in all subtypes of influenza-virus, that do not change from year to year, and that can be made available to the entire world population. We need an international approach to public funding that will pay for the excess production capacity required during a pandemic.

Today, public health experts and infectious-disease scientists do not know whether H5N1 avian influenza-virus threatens an imminent pandemic. Most indications, however, suggest that it is just a matter of time: witness the increasing number of H5N1 infections in humans and animals, the documentation of additional small clusters of cases suggestive of near misses with respect to sustained human-to-human transmission, the ongoing genetic changes in the H5N1 Z genotype that have increased its pathogenicity, and the existence in Asia of a genetic-reassortment laboratory—the mix of an unprecedented number of people, pigs, and poultry.

It is sobering to realize that in 1968, when the most recent influenza pandemic occurred, the virus emerged in a China that had a human population of 790 million, a pig population of 5.2 million, and a poultry population of 12.3 million; today, these populations number 1.3 billion, 508 million, and 13 billion, respectively. Similar changes have occurred in the human and animal populations of other Asian countries, creating an incredible mixing vessel for viruses. Given this reality, as well as the exponential growth in foreign travel during the past 50 years, we must accept that a pandemic is coming—although whether it will be caused by H5N1 or by another novel strain remains to be seen.

Should H5N1 become the next pandemic strain, the resultant morbidity and mortality could rival those of 1918, when more than half the deaths occurred among largely healthy people between 18 and 40 years of age and were caused by a virus-induced cytokine storm that led to the acute respiratory distress syndrome (ARDS).[4] The ARDS-related morbidity and mortality in the pandemic of 1918 was on a different scale from those of 1957 and 1968—a fact that highlights the importance of the virulence of the virus subtype or genotype. Clinical, epidemiologic, and laboratory evidence suggests that a pandemic caused by the current H5N1 strain would be more likely to mimic the 1918 pandemic than those that occurred

Protecting Against a Pandemic

My administration has developed a comprehensive national strategy, with concrete measures we can take to prepare for an influenza pandemic. . . . First, we must detect outbreaks that occur anywhere in the world; second, we must protect the American people by stockpiling vaccines and antiviral drugs, and improve our ability to rapidly produce new vaccines against a pandemic strain; and, third, we must be ready to respond at the federal, state and local levels in the event that a pandemic reaches our shores.

George W. Bush, "President Outlines Pandemic Influenza Preparations and Response," The White House, November 1, 2005. www.whitehouse.gov/news/releases/2005/11/20051101-1.html.

A yearly flu shot is recommended to stop the spread of the virus, helping to eliminate mass contamination of the strain from person to person.

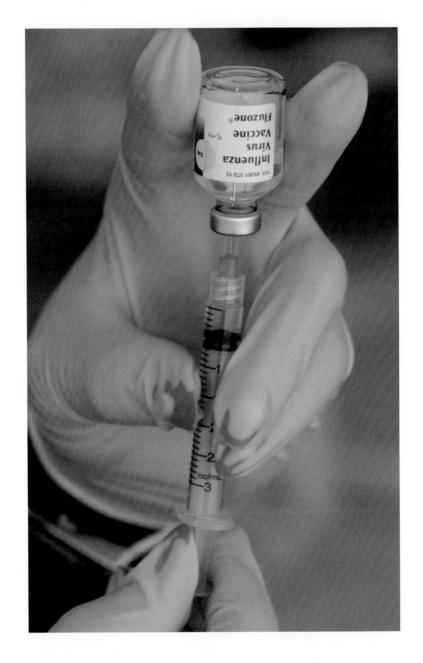

more recently.[5] If we translate the rate of death associated with the 1918 influenzavirus to that in the current population, there could be 1.7 million deaths in the United States and 180 million to 360 million deaths globally. We have an extremely limited armamentarium with which to handle millions of cases of ARDS—one not much different from that available to the front-line medical corps in 1918.

Is there anything we can do to avoid this course? The answer is a qualified yes that depends on how everyone, from world leaders to local elected officials, decides to respond. We need bold and timely leadership at the highest levels of the governments in the developed world; these governments must recognize the economic, security, and health threats posed by the next influenza pandemic and invest accordingly. The resources needed must be considered in the light of the eventual costs of failing to invest in such an effort. The loss of human life even in a mild pandemic will be devastating, and the cost of a world economy in shambles for several years can only be imagined.

Analyze the essay:

1. In discussing the challenges society would face if struck by a pandemic, Osterholm lists the "just-in-time delivery" economy as a major contributor to disaster and chaos. What does he mean by this?

2. Osterholm discusses how in the event of a pandemic, health care centers would be overrun. He predicts that health care workers would experience death tolls equal to or higher than the public, and some may abandon their posts completely. What suggestions might you make to fix this problem? If you were in charge, how would you go about readying the health care industry to deal with a health disaster on the scale of a pandemic?

Notes

1. Johnson NP, Mueller J. Updating the account global mortality of the 1918-1920 "Spanish" influenza pandemic. Bull Hist Med 2002;76:105-15.

2. Stöhr K. Avian influenza and pandemics—research needs and opportunities. N Engl J Med 2005;352:405-7.

3. Sandman PM, Lanard J. Pandemic influenza risk communication: the teachable moment. 2005. (Assessed April 14, 2005, at http://www.psandman.com/col/pandemic.htm.)

4. Kobasa D, Takada A, Shinya K, et al. Enhanced virulence of influenza A viruses with haemagglutinin of the 1918 pandemic virus. Nature 2004;431:703-7.

5. Peiris JS, Yu WC, Leung CW, et al. Re-emergence of fatal human influenza A subtype H5N1 disease. Lancet 2004;363:617-9.

Efforts to Prevent a Pandemic May Cause a Pandemic

Wendy Orent

In the following essay Wendy Orent warns that experiments on pandemic-causing flu strains may accidentally cause a new pandemic. She discusses how researchers have all but re-created a strain of flu that caused the 1918 Spanish flu pandemic. She worries that the strain they have re-created could be mishandled, accidentally fall into the wrong hands, or be acquired by bioterrorists. The research is not carried out under the highest biosafety security levels, meaning that researchers are not required to take the utmost precautions when handling their deadly work. Furthermore, Orent questions the need for such research in the first place, as it seems largely academic. Orent warns that the next flu pandemic may strike as a result of human error rather than natural evolution.

Orent is the author of *Plague: The Mysterious Past and Terrifying Future of the World's Most Dangerous Disease.*

Consider the following questions:

1. What mistake did Meridian Bioscience make with a pandemic flu strain? How does the example support the author's argument?
2. What is the Western Front, and how did it provide ideal conditions for the 1918 flu pandemic?
3. What fatal mistakes have researchers made when handling deadly biological agents, as reported by Orent?

Flu used to be the "Rodney Dangerfield of diseases," as Tim Uyeki puts it. Uyeki is a flu epidemiologist at the Centers for Disease Control and Prevention (CDC) in Atlanta, and he's been concerned that for years people didn't give influenza the respect it deserved.

But now flu has all the attention any germ can get. First, there was a flu vaccine shortage over the winter, prompting long lines and provoking rage from people who couldn't get their shots. Later, bird flu mesmerized the world, with the CDC and the World Health Organization (WHO) keeping up a steady drumbeat: A flu pandemic—overdue for decades—would be upon us at any moment. Finally, it was announced that a pandemic flu strain had been accidentally sent to influenza labs around the world as part of a testing kit by Meridian Bioscience, a contractor for the College of American Pathologists.

The jittery WHO, poised for catastrophe, insisted on the immediate destruction of the strain, for fear of accidental release. And while the threat posed by Meridian's error is far less than initial reports suggested, the reality is that lab accidents do happen. What's more, the feverish anxiety of public health officials to head off a new influenza pandemic may be generating the greatest influenza threat we face.

Scientists May Accidentally Unleash a Plague

The threat is man-made. Scientists in the United States and Great Britain are studying the deadliest flu epidemic of the last century, the 1918 pandemic. In order to learn what made it kill so many, they are working on producing artificial viruses that replace common human flu genes with 1918 genes. An accidental release of one of their constructs could make the Meridian error look as menacing as a cauliflower.

The flu strain sent out by Meridian is known as H2N2/Japan. H2N2 strains first appeared in 1957, causing a world-wide pandemic. But H2N2/Japan is what virologists call a "reference reagent," regularly used in laboratory tests. It's already in the freezers of every serious flu researcher, says virologist Earl Brown of the University of Ottawa. Furthermore, calling the H2N2/Japan strain a "killer"—as news reports across the globe have done— makes little sense. It is no deadlier than any other new strain, and may actually be less so. According to microbiologist and pathologist Jared N. Schwartz, of the College of American Pathologists, H2N2/Japan has been through lab processes that typically weaken the virus. No one has contracted H2N2/Japan from these lab kits. This is not surprising. As flu researcher Adolfo Garcia-Sastre of the

Some fear that experimental flu strains could cause a global pandemic outbreak if not properly handled.

Mount Sinai School of Medicine in New York puts it, you'd have to aerosolize the virus in some way in order to catch it—not something that is likely to be done with a reference strain.

Following the pandemic of 1957, which killed perhaps a million people, most of them elderly, H2N2 became the dominant human flu virus for 11 years. In 1968, a new strain, called H3N2, caused a new pandemic, and H2N2 mysteriously vanished. People born after 1968 may have partial immunity because of the N2 component of the virus, common also to the currently circulating H3N2 strain. Still, no one born after 1968 has full immunity, so WHO flu experts are concerned that a lab accident could cause another pandemic. But H2N2, like most flu strains, is disproportionately deadly to the elderly—precisely the group most likely to have some immunity.

The WHO's frenzied demands that laboratories destroy this strain seem like an overreaction. Apparently, WHO wants to show a nervous world that it is taking action. But this mania to do something—anything—to stave off a pandemic has been building for years and led to the imprudent decision to re-create the dangerous 1918 strain.

Using Science to Re-Create the Past

The 1918 flu evolved its lethality on World War I's Western Front. This was no accident. According to Carol Byerly, a historian of military medicine and author of a new book, *Fever of War: The Influenza Epidemic in the U.S. Army During World War I*, the 1918 flu built up its unique virulence in the trenches and the hospitals, the trains and trucks of the front, where the deathly ill lay beside the uninfected, allowing lethal strains to be easily passed on.

Tissue samples that prescient World War I Army physicians stored away, combined with flu RNA taken from the partially frozen corpse of an Inuit woman in

Brevig Mission, Alaska, have yielded enough genetic information to allow the sequencing of all eight genes in the 1918 influenza virus genome. Molecular pathologist Jeffery Taubenberger and his colleagues from the Armed Forces Institute of Pathology have brought these lost genes from 1918 back from the dead; they've sequenced five of the genes, and are close to completing the last three as well.

These sequences by themselves are harmless: They are strings of information. As Garcia-Sastre puts it, "There's no smoking gun in the 1918 sequences. So we really want to find out what made it kill, so that if it emerges again in the future, we'd be able to recognize a virus with virulence characteristics like 1918." Through a technique Garcia-Sastre and colleagues developed, these sequences—symbols on paper—can be translated into actual viral RNA. Since the whole genome hasn't yet been published, scientists can't recreate the entire 1918 flu. But they can combine some 1918 genes either with laboratory strains that have been adapted to grow in mice, which don't normally catch human flu, or with ordinary human flu strains to yield new artificial strains. Then the researcher infects mice with his new strain. Strains using three of the 1918 genes are already known to kill mice.

Looking for a Gas Leak with a Lighted Match

These techniques are fascinating. But the work is also dangerous. Peter B. Jahrling, chief scientist at the National Institute of Allergy and Infectious Diseases, compares the

Could Terrorists Acquire a Flu Strain?

Since 9/11, the specter of bioterrorism looms over almost every infectious event, although every indication suggests there were no villains, just a lack of communication between different members of an increasingly disjointed public health network [which accidentally sent a top secret deadly strain of flu to five thousand laboratories in eighteen countries]. In the United States, there is no government regulation over the 1957 flu strain. In fact, federal officials at the CDC do not even know how many U.S. laboratories keep this deadly strain in their "viral libraries."

Howard Markel, "The Flu Snafu—the Story Behind Strain A (H2N2)," *Globalist*, April 18, 2005. www.theglobalist.com/dbweb/StoryId.aspx?StoryId = 4502.

research to "looking for a gas leak with a lighted match." What concerns Jahrling and Brown, among others, is that experiments involving 1918 genes are not being carried out under the highest biosafety level, BSL-4. While most of the scientists use what is known as BSL-3 plus, or enhanced, conditions, they do not use space suits, chemical showers or gas-tight cabinets in their work.

Still, it's hard to say how much difference a higher biosafety level would make: Work on dangerous agents is, by definition, dangerous. Even in BSL-4 labs mistakes can happen, and some of these mistakes have been fatal—to the experimenter. In addition to three laboratory escapes of the SARS virus in 2003 and several resultant fatalities, a number of Russian researchers at the Vektor laboratories in Siberia have died of Ebola, and several scientists at Boston University contracted tularemia, or rabbit fever, in recent years.

CDC research scientist Dr. Terrence Tumpey discusses work on the re-creation of the 1918 pandemic bird flu virus in October 2005. Tumpey and others believe that bioterrorists might be able to use such viral strains to cause a worldwide pandemic.

Needless Research Could Give Rise to a Deadly Accident—or Bioterrorism

The 1918 flu is a particularly potent agent, and it isn't only the lives of experimenters at risk if one of them contracts one of the artificial constructs. As Brown puts it, "These are tried and true virulence strains for humans. This virus and its genes have to be given a bit more respect. You don't want it out in nature where it could cause serious disease." While the antiviral drug oseltamivir, or Tamiflu, seems to protect against the 1918 constructs, Jahrling says "you'd really want a belt to go with those suspenders." And Richard Ebright, a microbiologist at Rutgers University, says that "using Tamiflu as a prophylactic makes it more likely that if a strain is accidentally released, it's going to be a Tamiflu-resistant strain."

There's an added danger. The scientists now known to be working on these strains are all respected by their peers; no one expects them to be careless. But the five published sequences are in the public domain, and there is simply no way to know who else may be working on them at any given time. Even more disturbing is what may happen when Taubenberger publishes the remaining three gene sequences. Then the entire 1918 flu could be built from scratch by anyone, anywhere, who has sufficient resources and skill. It is quite conceivable that resurrected 1918 flu could someday be used as a bioterrorist agent.

Unnecessary Research Causes Unnecessary Risk

Clearly, if these genes had never been dug up, we wouldn't have to worry about any of this. And how necessary is this admittedly remarkable work in the first place? Evolutionary biologist Paul Ewald of the University of Louisville points out that influenza is normally a relatively mild disease: It keeps its hosts up and moving in order for it to spread. But the precise conditions of the Western Front allowed the virus to evolve unprecedented virulence.

Without those conditions, lethal pandemic flu cannot evolve. Says Byerly, "The 1918 flu epidemic most likely will not happen again because we won't construct the Western Front again."

If Ewald and Byerly are right, then the principal rationale for this research—protection from another lethal pandemic—blows away, though the research remains a useful tool to show how lethal flu kills.

Indeed, if they are right, the greatest danger of lethal pandemic flu may lie in some slip, some failure of lab protocol or Tamiflu, or even in someone's malice. Then the vaunted cure may prove worse than the disease.

Analyze the essay:

1. Orent quotes from several sources to support the points she makes in her essay. Make a list of everyone she quotes, including their credentials and the nature of their comments. Then analyze her sources—are they credible? Are they well qualified to speak on this subject?

2. Orent says she worries that someone might re-create a pandemic flu strain and use it in a bioterrorist attack. How likely do you think this scenario is? What precautions might you suggest laboratories, scientists, and world leaders take to avoid such a scenario from occurring?

Section Two:
Model Essays
and Writing
Excercises

The Five-Paragraph Essay

An *essay* is a short piece of writing that discusses or analyzes one topic. The five-paragraph essay is a form commonly used in school assignments and tests. Every five-paragraph essay begins with an *introduction*, ends with a *conclusion*, and features three *supporting paragraphs* in the middle.

The Thesis Statement. The introduction includes the essay's thesis statement. The thesis statement presents the argument or point the author is trying to make about the topic. The essays in this book all have different thesis statements because they each make different arguments or points about pandemics.

The thesis statement should clearly tell the reader what the essay will be about. A focused thesis statement helps determine what will be in the essay; the subsequent paragraphs are spent developing and supporting its argument.

The Introduction. In addition to presenting the thesis statement, a well-written introductory paragraph captures the attention of the reader and explains why the topic being explored is important. It may provide the reader with background information on the subject matter or feature an anecdote that illustrates a point relevant to the topic. It could also present startling information that clarifies the point of the essay or put forth a contradictory position that the essay will refute. Further techniques for writing an introduction are found later in this section.

The Supporting Paragraphs. The introduction is then followed by three (or more) supporting paragraphs. These are the main body of the essay. Each paragraph presents and develops a subtopic that supports the essay's thesis statement. Each subtopic is spearheaded by a *topic sentence* and supported by its own facts, details, and examples. The writer can use various kinds of supporting material and details to back up the topic of each supporting paragraph. These may include statistics, quotations from people with special knowledge or expertise, historic facts, and anecdotes. A rule of writing is that specific and concrete examples are more convincing than vague, general, or unsupported assertions.

The Conclusion. The conclusion is the paragraph that closes the essay. Its function is to summarize or reiterate the main idea of the essay. It may recall an idea from the introduction or briefly examine the larger implications of the thesis. Because the conclusion is also the last chance a writer has to make an impression on the reader, it is important that it not simply repeat what has been presented elsewhere in the essay but close it in a clear, final, and memorable way.

Although the order of the essay's component paragraphs is important, they do not have to be written in the order presented here. Some writers like to decide on a thesis and write the introduction paragraph first. Other writers like to focus first on the body of the essay and write the introduction and conclusion later.

Pitfalls to Avoid

When writing essays about controversial issues such as pandemics, it is important to remember that disputes over the material are common precisely because there are many different perspectives. Remember to state your arguments in careful and measured terms. Evaluate your topic fairly—avoid overstating negative qualities of one perspective or understating positive qualities of another. Use examples, facts, and details to support any assertions you make.

The Expository Essay

The previous section of this book provided you with samples of writings on pandemics. All made arguments or advocated a particular position about pandemics and related topics. All included elements of *expository* writing as well. The purpose of expository writing is to inform the reader about a particular subject matter. Sometimes a writer will use exposition simply to communicate knowledge; other times, he or she will use exposition to persuade a reader to accept a particular point of view.

Types of Expository Writing

There are several different types of expository writing: definition, classification, process, illustration, and problem/solution. Examples of these types can be found in the viewpoints in the preceding chapter. The list below provides some ideas on how exposition could be organized and presented. Each type of writing could be used separately or in combination in five-paragraph essays.

Definition. Definition refers to simply telling what something is. Definitions can be encompassed in a sentence or paragraph. At other times, definitions may take a paragraph or more. The act of defining some topics—especially abstract concepts—can sometimes serve as the focus of entire essays. An example of definition is found in Viewpoint Two by Peter M. Sandman. He opens his essay by defining pandemics, explaining they are random events that cannot be "overdue." Similarly, in Viewpoint Three author Pat Jackson Allen provides a definition of avian influenza so readers can follow her analysis of it in the rest of the essay.

Classification. A classification essay describes and clarifies relationships between things by placing them in different categories, based on their similarities and differences. This can be a good way of organizing and presenting information.

Process. A process essay looks at how something is done. The writer presents events in a chronological or ordered sequence of steps. Process writing can either inform the reader of a past event or process by which something was made, or instruct the reader on how to do something.

Illustration. Illustration is one of the simplest and most common patterns of expository writing. Simply put, it explains by giving specific and concrete examples. It is an effective technique for making one's writing both more interesting and more intelligible. An example of illustration is found in Viewpoint One by Michael Leavitt. He uses illustration when he gives specific and concrete examples of ways in which the government has prepared for a pandemic.

Problem/Solution. Problem/solution refers to when the author raises a problem or a question, then uses the rest of the paragraph or essay to answer the question or provide possible resolutions to the problem. It can be an effective way of drawing in the reader while imparting information. Michael T. Osterholm, the author of Viewpoint Five, for example, uses problem/solution to argue that a multipronged approach is required to prevent a pandemic. He raises the problem of an impending pandemic and proposes solving that problem by installing a variety of complementary emergency preparedness programs.

Words and Phrases Common to Expository Essays

Writers use these words and phrases to explain their subjects, to provide transitions between paragraphs, and to summarize key ideas in an essay's concluding paragraph.

accordingly	from this perspective	it seems as though
because	furthermore	it then follows that
clearly	evidently	moreover
consequently	however	since
first . . . second . . .	indeed	subsequently
third . . .	it is important to under-	therefore
for example	stand	this is why
for this reason	it makes sense to	thus

What Makes a Pandemic?

Editor's Notes One way of writing an expository essay is to use the "definition" method. Definition refers to simply telling what something is. Definitions take up a sentence, a paragraph, or even a whole essay. This is what the first model essay does—it uses the definition method to define what pandemics are. In doing so, it offers the reader a more specific glimpse into what causes pandemics, how they spread, and how they can be cured.

As you read this essay, pay attention to its components and how it is organized. Also note that all sources are cited using Modern Language Association (MLA) style.* For more information on how to cite your sources see Appendix C. In addition, consider the following questions:

1. How does the introduction engage the reader's attention?
2. What pieces of supporting evidence are used to back up the essay's arguments?
3. What purpose do the essay's quotes serve?
4. How does the author transition from one idea to another?

Paragraph 1

Almost every day it seems there is a story in the news about pandemics. Politicians, scientists, physicians, policy makers, and other concerned voices are all talking about the possibility of a disease that could become a pandemic. But what exactly is a pandemic disease? When studying

---

*In applying MLA style guidelines in this book, the following simplifications have been made: Parenthetical text citations are confined to direct quotations only; electronic source documentation in the Works Cited list omits date of access, page ranges, and some detailed facts of publication.

pandemics it is important to realize that not just any disease is capable of becoming pandemic. All pandemic diseases share a few basic qualities, such as being able to spread far distances, kill high numbers of people, be new to the human immune system, and be transmittable from human to human.

This is the essay's thesis statement. It previews what topics the author will discuss.

Paragraph 2

One feature of pandemic diseases is their ability to spread through human populations across regions such as continents. Especially serious pandemics are even able to spread across the globe. The 1918–1919 Spanish flu pandemic, for example, ripped through countries in North America, Europe, Asia, Africa, Latin America, and the Arctic and even hit remote islands scattered across the South Pacific. In addition to spreading near and far, pandemic diseases work quickly, too. The 1918–1919 pandemic killed 50 to 100 million people in as little time as a year and a half.

This is the topic sentence of paragraph 2. This paragraph will stay focused on this idea.

This is a supporting detail. This information directly supports the topic sentence helping to prove it true.

Paragraph 3

Another feature of pandemic diseases is that they are new to the human population. They move quickly and kill so many because humans, having no previous exposure to the diseases, lack immunity. According to the World Health Organization (WHO), influenza pandemics in particular occur when "a new influenza virus subtype emerges." In other words, though previous strains of influenza have caused pandemics (H1N1 is believed to have caused the 1918 Spanish flu pandemic, for example), a new pandemic would need to be caused by a strain of flu that humans have not yet encountered. Experts at the WHO and elsewhere worry that the flu strain H5N1, known as avian influenza or "bird flu," could be such a strain. In fact, the WHO has confirmed that the H5N1 virus is "a new virus for humans (H5N1 viruses have never circulated widely among people). No one will have immunity should an H5N1-like pandemic virus emerge."

What is the topic sentence of paragraph 3? How did you recognize it?

The WHO is a credible source that can speak with authority on the subject. Only quote credible sources in your essays.

"In other words" and "In fact" are transitional phrases that keep the ideas in the essay moving. Make a list of all transitional words and phrases used in the essay.

This is the topic sentence of paragraph 4. Note how it supports the essay's thesis. Also note how everything in paragraph 4 serves to further explain this point.

This fact was taken from Appendix A in this book. This book contains many resources for writing an essay on pandemics.

This quote was taken from Viewpoint One. As you research, jot down quotes that could be used to support points you make in your essays.

Note how the conclusion returns to the main idea put forth by the essay's thesis.

Paragraph 4

A final feature of pandemic diseases is their ability to spread from person to person. All modern diseases that have the ability to transform into pandemics—the Ebola virus, Lassa fever, Rift Valley fever, Marburg virus, Bolivian hemorrhagic fever, the HIV virus, and the SARS virus—are also able to be transmitted from human to human. Diseases such as cancer, on the other hand, may sicken and kill many people, but because cancer is not spread from person to person, it is not considered to be pandemic. One disease experts say is most likely to turn pandemic—the H5N1 avian influenza—has not yet demonstrated the capacity to jump from human to human, but it could in the near future. The human deaths caused thus far by H5N1 were transmitted to humans by livestock such as chickens. However, previous influenzas, such as the 1918 strain, became pandemic precisely when the strain mutated and developed the ability to jump from human to human. Scientists worry that if an influenza strain mutated in the past, H5N1 could mutate in the future: "We've been able to use reversed genetics to identify that that virus, the 1918 virus, has great similarity to the H5N1 virus that we now see spread across the world. Should it achieve human-to-human transmissibility [the way the Spanish flu did] . . . it would be an aggressive killer. That's why we're concerned" (Leavitt).

Paragraph 5

Not all diseases are capable of becoming pandemic. Those that have the ability to wreak havoc, death, and sickness across the globe all share a few basic characteristics. Understanding the features of pandemic diseases goes a long way in recognizing when a disease could possibly turn pandemic—and thus helps humanity prepare for the next one.

Works Cited

"Avian Influenza: Frequently Asked Questions." *World Health Organization* 5 Dec. 2005 < www.who.int/csr/ disease/avian_influenza/avian_faqs/en/ > .

Leavitt, Michael. "We're Overdue for a Pandemic." *U.S. News & World Report* 20 Apr. 2006.

Exercise 1A: Create an Outline from an Existing Essay

It often helps to create an outline of the five-paragraph essay before you write it. The outline can help you organize the information, arguments, and evidence you have gathered during your research.

For this exercise, create an outline that could have been used to write "What Makes a Pandemic?" Identify topic sentences and provide at least two supporting details for each sentence. This "reverse engineering" exercise is meant to help familiarize you with how outlines can help classify and arrange information.

To do this you will need to
1. articulate the essay's thesis,
2. pinpoint important pieces of evidence,
3. flag quotes that support the essay's ideas, and
4. identify key points that support the argument.

Part of the outline has already been started to give you an idea of the assignment.

Outline

I. Paragraph 1:

    A. Write the essay's thesis: All pandemic diseases share a few basic qualities.

II. Paragraph 2 topic:

    A.

    B. The 1918–1919 pandemic killed 50 to 100 million people in as little time as a year and a half.

III. Paragraph 3 topic:

    A. A new pandemic would need to be caused by a strain of flu that humans have not yet encountered.

B. WHO quote about how humans do not have immunity to H5N1.

IV. Paragraph 4 topic:

A. All modern diseases that have the ability to transform into pandemics—the Ebola virus, Lassa fever, Rift Valley fever, Marburg virus, Bolivian hemorrhagic fever, the HIV virus, and the SARS virus—are also able to be transmitted from human to human.

B.

V. Paragraph 5:

A. Write the essay's conclusion:

Essay Two

Preparing for a Pandemic Is a Win-Win Situation

Editor's Notes Another way of writing an expository essay is to use the "problem/solution" method. Problem/solution refers to when the author raises a problem or a question and then uses the rest of the paragraph or essay to answer the question or provide solutions to the problem.

The second model essay uses problem/solution to argue that the United States should prepare for a pandemic. The author identifies three problems—the fragility of America's medical infrastructure; the unemployment rate; and the threat of pandemic or terrorist attack—that could all be solved by taking such preparations.

This essay differs from the other model essays in this section in that it is persuasive. Rather than merely explaining an issue, idea, or event, it attempts to convince the reader of a particular point of view. While exposition is a good medium for neutral or informational essays, it can also work for essays in which the author wants to argue a point.

As you did with the first essay, use the notes in the margins to figure out how this essay is organized and written.

The author opens the essay by establishing a problem—the inability of the medical system to cope with a pandemic. The solution is to update the system. The rest of the essay will focus on other problems that would be solved by preparing for a pandemic.

Paragraph 1

Preparing for a pandemic would require America to update its medical system. More health care specialists, materials, facilities, and equipment would be needed to treat the thousands of people who would be sickened every day by a deadly virus that spreads like wildfire through the population. Secretary of Health and Human Services Michael Leavitt predicts that if a pandemic were to strike the United States today, "45 million Americans would become sick enough that they would require some kind of serious medical attention, whether that was a clinic visit or hospital stay." Clearly, much needs to be done to prepare for such a disaster. Surprisingly, people often debate whether preparing for a pandemic makes sense given the nation's limited resources and uncertainty over whether a deadly disease is actually likely to strike the United States. But it is important to realize that in addition to making sure Americans have resources in a time of medical crisis, pandemic preparations would solve several problems faced in America today.

Paragraph 2

In addition to preparing us for a pandemic, upgrading the nation's medical infrastructure would help solve another pressing problem faced by Americans today—the threat from terrorism. Indeed, hospitals and trauma centers are currently unable to accommodate the volume of victims expected to be produced by a large-scale terrorist attack. This fact is a huge concern among those who deal in counterterrorism tactics. In fact, the number one objective of the Food and Drug Administration's counterterrorism agenda is to "facilitate the development and availability of medical countermeasures to limit the effects of a terrorist attack on the civilian or military populations. Medical products (human and animal drugs, vaccines and other biological products, blood and blood products, medical devices) must be readily available to prevent, diagnose, and treat illnesses resulting from a terrorist attack. In addition, specialized products could be needed for certain groups, such as military personnel, first responders to emergencies, residents near nuclear facilities, pregnant women, immunocompromised persons, and children." Every single one of these resources would be needed in the event of a pandemic, too. By preparing for a pandemic, we can simultaneously prepare for a terrorist attack, solving two problems with one initiative.

In making these preparations, another of America's pressing problems could be solved: increasing job insecurity and an ongoing unemployment rate. Indeed, hundreds of people are laid off every day due to outsourcing to overseas companies and increasing production expenses due to the higher cost of oil. Improvements to the medical industry to prepare for a pandemic, however, could create thousands of new jobs in health care, construction, and biotechnology. Government subsidies should help pay for the construction and salaries of this much-needed workforce. Much like it is the government's responsibility to fund schools and staff them with teachers, it should also be the government's responsibility to build hospitals and staff them with doctors and nurses who can take care of the population in the event of an emergency.

Paragraph 4

Finally, planning for a pandemic can help improve the performance of nearly every industry in America. By streamlining operations, generating emergency contingency plans, and preparing to protect both workers and products from the global shutdown that would arise from a pandemic, industries can help their business run smoother and faster and protect them from other upsets unrelated to pandemics. For example, if businesses have contingency plans for keeping in contact or maintaining delivery of their products, they are more likely to survive an emergency such as a natural disaster, terrorist attack, or oil shortage in addition to surviving a pandemic. For this reason, the director of the Center for Infectious Disease Research and Policy says, "Planning for a pandemic must be on the agenda of every public health agency, school board, manufacturing plant, investment firm, mortuary, state legislature, and food distributor" (Osterholm 1841).

What is the topic sentence of paragraph 3? How does it relate to the essay's thesis?

The author is expressing an opinion in these sentences. Opinions are a clue that an essay is persuasive—that is, the author is trying to convince you of a point of view.

This is the topic sentence of paragraph 4. Note that although it still relates to the essay's thesis, it is a new topic that hasn't been raised in another paragraph.

"For example" is a transitional phrase that helps keep the ideas in the essay flowing. Make a list of all transitional words and phrases used in the essay.

This quote was taken from Viewpoint Five. Remember to incorporate quotes from credible sources into the essays you write.

Of course, it is hoped that preparations for a pandemic are never needed. But hoping and wishing offer no protection in crisis. Americans must take any precautions that will help them survive if a pandemic were to strike. There is no downside to this plan, for even if a pandemic never strikes, the upgrades to the medical care system, the job market, and protections against other threats such as terrorism will be well worth it. As Secretary of Health and Human Services Michael Leavitt notes, "Even if a pandemic does not happen soon, we'll be a stronger and a healthier nation because the pandemic preparation is the same preparation that we would make for a bioterrorism event. It's the same preparation that we would make for a medical disaster brought on by a natural consequence, like a hurricane or a tornado." So let's prepare for a pandemic—we have nothing to lose, and everything to gain.

Note how this thought captures the heart of the essay's thesis without repeating what has already been stated.

Note that Leavitt's comment (taken from Viewpoint One) directly supports the essay's main thesis. Only use quotes that are relevant to points you make.

Works Cited

"Counterterrorism: Protecting America from Terrorism." Food and Drug Administration < http://www.fda.gov/oc/mcclellan/strategic_terrorism.html > .

Leavitt, Michael. "We're Overdue for a Pandemic." *U.S. News & World Report* 20 Apr. 2006.

Osterholm, Michael T. "Preparing for the Next Pandemic." *New England Journal of Medicine* 5 May 2005: 1839–1842.

Exercise 2A: Create an Outline from an Existing Essay

As you did for the first model essay in this section, create an outline that could have been used to write "Preparing for a Pandemic Is a Win-Win Situation." Be sure to identify the essay's thesis statement, its supporting ideas, and key pieces of evidence that were used.

Exercise 2B: Create an Outline for Your Own Essay

The second model essay expresses a particular point of view about pandemics. For this exercise, your assignment is to find supporting ideas, choose specific and concrete details, create an outline, and ultimately write a five-paragraph essay making a different, or even opposing, point about pandemics. Your goal is to use expository techniques to convince your reader.

Part I: Write a thesis statement.

The following thesis statement would be appropriate for an opposing essay on why preparing for pandemics is not a win-win situation:

Preparing for a pandemic that is unlikely ever to strike is a waste of precious resources and unnecessarily panics the public.

Or see the sample paper topics suggested in Appendix D for more ideas.

Part II: Brainstorm pieces of supporting evidence.

Using information from some of the viewpoints in the previous section and from the information found in Section Three of this book, write down three arguments or pieces of evidence that support the thesis statement you selected. Then, for each of these three arguments, write down supportive facts, examples, and details that support it. These could be:

- statistical information;
- facts;
- unique opinions;
- appeals to logic, reason, or emotion;
- quotes or anecdotes from experts or others with knowledge;
- observations of people's actions and behaviors;
- specific and concrete details.

Supporting pieces of evidence for the above sample topic sentence are found in this book and include:

- Points made in Viewpoint Two by Peter Sandman on how it is impossible for a pandemic to be "overdue," and unnecessarily preparing for one erodes the public's trust in government.
- Points made in Viewpoint Four by Michael Fumento on how a bird flu pandemic is not likely to occur anytime soon.
- Quote accompanying Viewpoint Two by Richard Schabas about how tuberculosis, malaria, and HIV kill millions of people each year, and there is no current pandemic. Devoting resources to protecting against a pandemic, therefore, is wasting money, research, and technology that could go toward fighting other, more threatening diseases.
- Quote accompanying Viewpoint Four by Peter Curson that discusses why spending money on pandemics is a waste of resources.

Part III: Place the information from Part II in outline form.

Part IV: Write the arguments or supporting statements in paragraph form.

By now you have three arguments that support the essay's thesis statement, as well as supporting material. Use the outline to write out your three supporting arguments in paragraph form. Make sure each paragraph has a topic sentence that states the paragraph's thesis clearly and broadly. Then add supporting sentences that express the facts, quotes, details, and examples that support the paragraph's argument. The paragraph may also have a concluding or summary sentence.

Learning from the 1918–1919 Spanish Flu Pandemic

Editor's Notes Yet another way of writing an expository essay is to use the "process" method. A process essay generally looks at how something is done. The writer presents events or steps in a chronological or ordered sequence. Process writing can either inform the reader of a past event, a process by which something was made, or tell a reader how to do something. The following model essay uses process to discuss the 1918–1919 Spanish influenza pandemic. The author explains step by step how the deadly virus moved around the globe and what factors facilitated its spread.

This essay also differs from previous ones in that it is longer than five paragraphs. Sometimes five paragraphs are simply not enough to develop an idea adequately. Extending the length of an essay can allow the reader to explore a topic in more depth or present multiple pieces of evidence that together provide a complete picture of a topic. Longer essays can also help readers discover the complexity of a subject by examining a topic beyond its superficial exterior. Moreover, the ability to write a sustained research or position paper is a valuable skill you will need as you advance academically.

As you read, consider the questions posed in the margins. Continue to identify thesis statements, supporting details, transitions, and quotations. Examine the introductory and concluding paragraphs to understand how they give shape to the essay. Finally, evaluate the essay's general structure and assess its overall effectiveness.

■ Refers to thesis and topic sentences

☐ Refers to supporting details

Paragraph 1

There was once an illness that spread so rapidly around the world, it killed between 50 and 100 million people in less than two years. This deadly pandemic was sparked by a microscopic strain of influenza that migrated from birds to humans. It ripped through the population so quickly that people died within days, even hours, of catching it. Studying the path of the 1918–1919 pandemic, otherwise known as the Spanish flu, is important for understanding just how devastating pandemics can be. It can also help us outline precautions that would need to be taken in the event of another pandemic.

What is the essay's thesis statement? [Hint: It is not the last sentence of paragraph 1.]

Paragraph 2

The world's worst pandemic began in the spring of 1918 in Army bases in the United States. It is believed that the very first case occurred on March 11 at Camp Funston, Kansas. An Army cook named Albert Mitchell came down with flu symptoms that included a fever, sore throat, headache, and aching muscles. By noon 107 soldiers reported feeling similar symptoms. After two days, more than 500 were sick. The flu spread from base to base, sickening thousands.

What features of this essay let you know it is describing a process?

Paragraph 3

Though soldiers were falling ill, the first wave of the Spanish flu went somewhat unnoticed given the political climate of the country. The United States had entered World War I; its troops were stationed across the globe, and news of flu outbreaks somewhat paled in comparison to news from the front lines. As one historian explains, "Few noticed the epidemic in the midst of the war, [President Woodrow] Wilson had just given his 14 point address [outlining war priorities]. There was virtually no response or acknowledgement to the epidemics in March and April in the military camps" (Billings). Other scholars note that because the epidemic went so unnoticed in the spring, the country—and the world—was unprepared when a second, deadlier wave of the Spanish flu struck later that year: "It was unfortunate that no steps were taken to prepare for the usual recrudescence of the viru-

What point does this quote directly support?

lent influenza strain in the winter. The lack of action was later criticized when the epidemic could not be ignored in the winter of 1918. These first epidemics at training camps were a sign of what was coming in greater magnitude in the fall and winter of 1918 to the entire world" (Billings).

Note how this information subtly supports the point made by the author in the essay's thesis: that lessons from the 1918–1919 pandemic can inform contemporary pandemic planning.

Paragraph 4

And spread it did—by the spring of 1918 the deadly influenza was on the move beyond the United States. In April it reached France, and a few weeks later showed up in China and Japan. By May the virus was sickening people in South America and Africa. It continued to travel through populations around the globe, and by the fall of 1918, a second wave of it appeared, this one more deadly than the last. The second wave probably developed in war trenches. Trench warfare was the main form of fighting in World War I; soldiers were stationed in trenches directly in the combat zone. Here they lived in extremely close and unsanitary conditions.

What is the topic sentence of paragraph 4? How did you recognize it?

Note how the story of how the pandemic spread is told using transitions that help ideas flow one into another. Aim for fluid, connected ideas when you write.

Paragraph 5

It was during this time that the virus made its way back to the United States. It reared its ugly head for a second time in Boston in September 1918. It is believed that the second wave of influenza returned to the United States via ships carrying supplies to and from war zones. Like the first wave, outbreaks in the second wave were initially seen in military camps (probably due to the close quarters and proximity to materials shipped from overseas). One man who witnessed the spread of the flu through military camps was Sergeant Charles L. Johnston, who served during World War I at Camp Funston. He nursed soldiers during the influenza epidemic. He wrote home to his wife about the spreading disease and its effects on the soldiers. In one letter, dated September 29, 1918, he wrote: "This has been a very long day indeed to me, for we are quarantined in for the time being. Have been for two days. We are held up because 'influenza,' or some such a name,

This type of quote is a *primary source* because it is from someone who personally experienced the pandemic. Primary sources enliven essays in many ways.

is in camp. It is some such a thing as pneumonia, and they seem to think it is pretty bad." Johnston witnessed and treated thousands of soldiers with the disease without ever succumbing to it himself.

Paragraph 6

What is the topic sentence of paragraph 6? What pieces of evidence directly support it?

The virus moved from the Army camps to the general population with speed and deadliness. Each day in the fall of 1918 came new reports of hundreds falling ill in cities such as Boston, Philadelphia, and New York. On a single October day, 851 New Yorkers died from the flu; residents of Philadelphia experienced death rates seven hundred times greater than normal. That month was so deadly that almost two hundred thousand Americans died from the flu in October 1918 alone! To this day, it remains the deadliest month in U.S. history.

Paragraph 7

Specific details such as these help your reader really picture the subject you are writing about. How do these details help you imagine what living through the pandemic was like?

The disease spread quickly in public gatherings of any type, such as parades, conferences, public hearings, city centers, and public transportation systems. Billings explains: "Stores could not hold sales, funerals were limited to 15 minutes. Some towns required a signed certificate to enter and railroads would not accept passengers without them. Those who ignored the flu ordinances had to pay steep fines enforced by extra officers." Public officials began providing face masks for protection. In San Francisco, for example, more than thirty thousand people who took to the streets to celebrate the end of World War I in November wore face masks to protect themselves.

Paragraph 8

What is the topic sentence of paragraph 8? How does it tie into the essay's thesis, which was put forth in paragraph 1?

Compounding the spread of the virus was the fact that the nation's health systems were unable to deal with a disaster of this magnitude. Hospitals and clinics experienced severe shortages of medical supplies and health care workers. Since many of the nation's doctors were tasked with tending to soldiers injured during the war, there were not enough physicians to treat the general population. It is reported that medical students stepped up to treat civilians, but they too were outnumbered by the number of people needing medical attention. With hundreds dying every day, the nation's health care system was also unequipped to deal with the number of dead bodies that needed to be processed. The system become flooded with corpses, and coffins, morticians, and gravediggers were in critical short supply.

Paragraph 9

The disease's spread elsewhere in the world was even more deadly. The flu strain was passed from country to country through trading routes, ships and other transportation, and military convoys. Outbreaks paralyzed nations in North America, Europe, Asia, Africa, Latin America, the South Pacific, even the Arctic. In some places the fatality rate was very high—in India, for example, 17 million people alone succumbed to the deadly flu. It is estimated that 60 percent of the Eskimo population was wiped out in Alaska, and islander populations such as the Samoans suffered infection rates as high as 80 to 90 percent.

What part of the "process" are we up to in paragraph 9? Has the author gone chronologically, telling the steps of the story in the right order?

Paragraph 10

By the time the pandemic was over in 1919, about a fifth, or 20 percent, of the world's population had become infected (more than a quarter, about 28 percent, of the U.S. population was infected). About 675,000 Americans died during the pandemic. The military was especially hard-hit—it is estimated that half of all U.S. soldiers who died in World War I succumbed to the Spanish flu, not to war wounds. Worldwide between 50 and 100 million people were killed. This staggering figure can be best understood by realizing "this extraordinary virus 'killed more people in a year than the Black Death of the Middle Ages killed in a century; it killed more people in twenty-four weeks than AIDS has killed in twenty four years'" (Allen 76).

In this paragraph the author starts bringing the story to a close by branching out and discussing the broad impact of the 1918–1919 pandemic.

This quote was taken from Viewpoint Three.

Paragraph 11

Also amazing is the fact that this frenzy of death and suffering took place in less than two years. Eighteen months after the Spanish flu first reared its ugly head, it disappeared from the face of the earth and has never circulated again. But the 1918–1919 pandemic remains what Secretary of Health and Human Services Michael Leavitt has called "the world's greatest medical disaster of all time." Experts such as Leavitt warn that if a disease even half as powerful as the Spanish flu were to spread around the globe today, tens of millions of people would fall ill, millions would die, and global trade and travel would halt. The 1918–1919 pandemic reminds us of the deadly effect pandemics can have on culture, politics, the economy, and the health of humans everywhere.

Remember to quote credible sources in your essays—it lends your points legitimacy.

The essay concludes by returning to its main point put forth in the introduction.

Works Cited

Allen, Pat Jackson. "Avian Influenza Pandemic: Not If, but When." *Pediatric Nursing* 10 Apr. 2006: 76–81.

Billings, Molly. "The Influenza Pandemic of 1918." Stanford University Feb. 2005 < www.stanford.edu/group/virus/uda/ > .

Johnston, Charles L. "Letter Dated Sunday, September 29, 1918." *Life at Camp Funston* < http://pages.suddenlink.net/tjohnston7/ww1hist/09-29-18.html > .

Leavitt, Michael. "We're Overdue for a Pandemic." *U.S. News & World Report* 20 Apr. 2006.

Exercise 3A: Examining Introductions and Conclusions

Every essay features introductory and concluding paragraphs that are used to frame the main ideas being presented. Along with presenting the essay's thesis statement, well-written introductions should grab the attention of the reader and make clear why the topic being explored is important. The conclusion reiterates the essay's thesis and is also the last chance for the writer to make an impression on the reader. Strong introductions and conclusions can greatly enhance an essay's effect on an audience.

The Introduction

There are several techniques that can be used to craft an introductory paragraph. An essay can start with

- an anecdote: a brief story that illustrates a point relevant to the topic;
- startling information: facts or statistics that elucidate the point of the essay;
- setting up and knocking down a position: a position or claim believed by proponents of one side of a controversy, followed by statements that challenge that claim;
- historical perspective: an example of the way things used to be that leads into a discussion of how or why things work differently now;
- summary information: general introductory information about the topic that feeds into the essay's thesis statement.

Problem One

Reread the introductory paragraphs of the model essays and of the viewpoints in Section One. Identify which of the techniques described above are used in the example essays. How do they grab the attention of the reader? Are their thesis statements clearly presented?

Problem Two
Write an introduction for the essay you have outlined and partially written in Exercise 2B using one of the techniques described above.

The Conclusion

The conclusion brings the essay to a close by summarizing or returning to its main ideas. Good conclusions, however, go beyond simply repeating these ideas. Strong conclusions explore a topic's broader implications and reiterate why they are important to consider. They may frame the essay by returning to an anecdote featured in the opening paragraph. Or they may close with a quotation or refer to an event in the essay. In opinionated essays, the conclusion can reiterate which side the essay is taking or ask the reader to reconsider a previously held position on the subject.

Problem Three
Reread the concluding paragraphs of the model essays and of the viewpoints in Section One. Which were most effective in driving their arguments home to the reader? What sorts of techniques did they use to do this? Did they appeal emotionally to the reader or bookend an idea or event referenced elsewhere in the essay?

Problem Four
Write a conclusion for the essay you have outlined and partially written in Exercise 2B using one of the techniques described above.

Author's Checklist

✔ Review the five-paragraph essay you wrote.
✔ Make sure it has a clear introduction that draws the reader in and contains a thesis statement that concisely expresses what your essay is about.

✔ Evaluate the paragraphs and make sure they each have clear topic sentences that are well supported by interesting and relevant details.

✔ Check that you have used compelling and authoritative quotes to enliven the essay.

✔ Finally, be sure you have a solid conclusion that uses one of the techniques presented in this exercise.

Exercise 3B: Using Quotations to Enliven Your Essay

No essay is complete without quotations. Get in the habit of using quotes to support at least some of the ideas in your essays. Quotes do not need to appear in every paragraph, but often enough so that the essay contains voices aside from your own. When you write, use quotations to accomplish the following:

- Provide expert advice that you are not necessarily in the position to know about
- Cite lively or passionate passages
- Include a particularly well-written point that gets to the heart of the matter
- Supply statistics or facts that have been derived from someone's research
- Deliver anecdotes that illustrate the point you are trying to make
- Express first-person testimony

Problem One
Reread the essays presented in all sections of this book and find at least one example of each of the above quotation types.

There are a couple of important things to remember when using quotations:

- Note your sources' qualifications and biases. This way your reader can identify the person you have quoted and can put their words in a context.
- Put any quoted material within proper quotation marks. Failing to attribute quotes to their authors constitutes plagiarism, which is when an author takes someone else's words or ideas and presents them as their own. Plagiarism is a very serious infraction and must be avoided at all costs.

Write Your Own Expository Five-Paragraph Essay

Using the information from this book, write your own five-paragraph expository essay that deals with a topic relating to pandemics. You can use the resources in this book for information about issues relating to this topic and how to structure this type of essay.

The following steps are suggestions on how to get started.

Step One: Choose your topic.

The first step is to decide what topic to write your expository essay on. Is there any subject that particularly fascinates you? Is there an issue you strongly support, or feel strongly against? Is there a topic you feel personally connected to or one that you would like to learn more about? Ask yourself such questions before selecting your essay topic. Refer to Appendix D: Sample Essay Topics if you need help selecting a topic.

Step Two: Write down questions and answers about the topic.

Before you begin writing, you will need to think carefully about what ideas your essay will contain. This is a process known as *brainstorming*. Brainstorming involves asking yourself questions and coming up with ideas to discuss in your essay. Possible questions that will help you with the brainstorming process include:

- Why is this topic important?
- Why should people be interested in this topic?
- How can I make this essay interesting to the reader?
- What question am I going to address in this paragraph or essay?
- What facts, ideas, or quotes can I use to support the answer to my question?

Questions especially for expository essays include:

- Do I want to write an informative essay or an opinionated essay?
- Will I need to explain a process or course of action?
- Will my essay contain many definitions or explanations?
- Is there a particular problem that needs to be solved?

Step Three: Gather facts, ideas, and anecdotes related to your topic.

This book contains several places to find information, including the viewpoints and the appendixes. In addition, you may want to research the books, articles, and Web sites listed in Section Three, or do additional research in your local library. You can also conduct interviews if you know someone who has a compelling story that would fit well in your essay.

Step Four: Develop a workable thesis statement.

Use what you have written down in steps two and three to help you articulate the main point or argument you want to make in your essay. It should be expressed in a clear sentence and make an arguable or supportable point.

Example:

Hysteria over the possibility of an impending pandemic erodes the public's trust in the government.

This could be the thesis statement of a persuasive expository essay that argues a pandemic is not likely to occur. Its central point would be that panic over pandemics should be avoided because it makes people lose trust in their government, which is dangerous in the event a real emergency were to occur.

Step Five: Write an outline or diagram.

1. Write the thesis statement at the top of the outline.
2. Write roman numerals I, II, and III on the left side of the page.

3. Next to each roman numeral, write down the best ideas you came up with in step three. These should all directly relate to and support the thesis statement.
4. Under each roman numeral list A, B, and C. Next to each letter write down information that supports that particular idea.

Step Six: Write the three supporting paragraphs.
Use your outline to write the three supporting paragraphs. Write down the main idea of each paragraph in sentence form. Do the same thing for the supporting points of information. Each sentence should support the paragraph of the topic. Be sure you have relevant and interesting details, facts, and quotes. Use transitions when you move from idea to idea to keep the text fluid and smooth. Sometimes, although not always, paragraphs can include a concluding or summary sentence that restates the paragraph's argument.

Step Seven: Write the introduction and conclusion.
See Exercise 3A for information on writing introductions and conclusions.

Step Eight: Read and rewrite.
As you read, check your essay for the following:

✔ Does the essay maintain a consistent tone?

✔ Do all paragraphs reinforce your general thesis?

✔ Do all paragraphs flow from one to the other? Do you need to add transition words or phrases?

✔ Have you quoted from reliable, authoritative, and interesting sources?

✔ Is there a sense of progression throughout the essay?

✔ Does the essay get bogged down in too much detail or irrelevant material?

✔ Does your introduction grab the reader's attention?

✔ Does your conclusion reflect on any previously discussed material, or give the essay a sense of closure?

✔ Are there any spelling or grammatical errors?

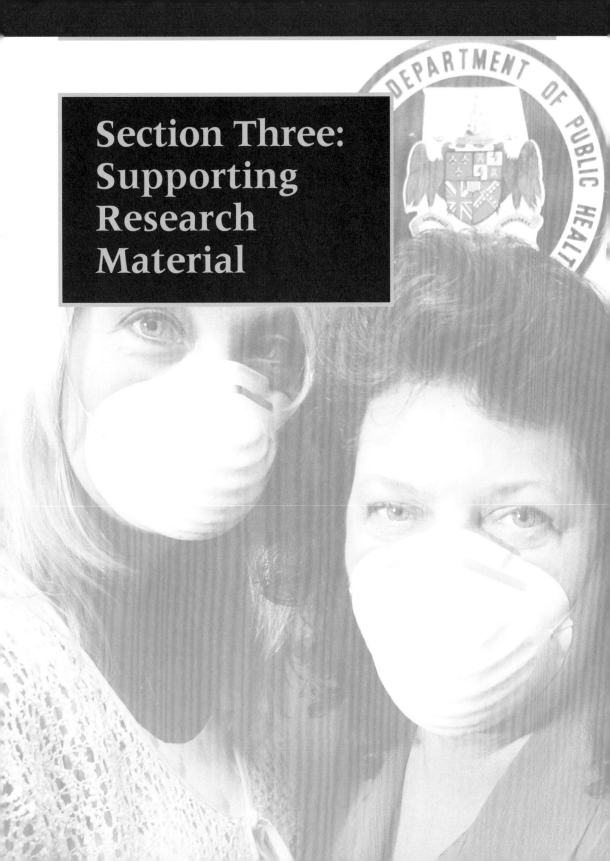

Section Three: Supporting Research Material

Facts About Pandemics

Editor's Note: These facts can be used in reports to reinforce or add credibility when making important points.

According to the World Health Organization:

- A pandemic is an epidemic that spreads through human populations across large regions, such as continents, or across the whole world.
- Pandemics can start when three conditions have been met: when a disease emerges that is new to the population; when the disease infects humans and causes serious illness; and when the disease spreads quickly and easily through humans.
- A pandemic is always transmittable from person to person (so, for example, though large numbers of people are infected with cancer it is not considered to be a pandemic disease).

  In recent history, major pandemics have occurred in:
  - 1729
  - 1732
  - 1781
  - 1830
  - 1833
  - 1889
  - 1918
  - 1957
  - 1968

  Scientists and health professionals are currently concerned that the following diseases have the potential to become pandemics:
  - Ebola virus
  - Lassa fever
  - Rift Valley fever

- Marburg virus
- Bolivian hemorrhagic fever
- HIV virus
- SARS virus
- Avian influenza

According to the U.S. government:

If a mild or moderate influenza pandemic, such as the one that spread in 1957 and 1968, were to break out in the United States:

- 90 million people, or 30 percent of the population, would fall ill
- 45 million, or 50 percent of those sickened, would need outpatient care
- 865,000 would need to be hospitalized
- 128,750 would need intensive care
- 64,875 would require a breathing apparatus
- 209,000 would die

If a severe influenza pandemic, such as the one that spread in 1918 and 1919, were to break out in the United States:

- 90 million people, or 30 percent of the population, would fall ill
- 45 million, or 50 percent of those sickened, would need outpatient care
- 9,900,000 would need to be hospitalized
- 1,485,000 would need intensive care
- 745,000 would require a breathing apparatus
- 1,903,000 would die

Facts about the 1918–1919 Spanish influenza:

- The 1918–1919 Spanish influenza killed between 50 million and 100 million people in under two years (about eighteen months).
- About a fifth, or 20 percent, of the world's population was infected.

- About 28 percent of the U.S. population was infected.
- About 675,000 Americans died during the pandemic, 10 times as many as in World War I.
- This deadly pandemic was sparked by a microscopic strain of influenza that migrated from birds to humans.
- Unlike most other strains of influenza, this strain mostly killed young adults. Ninety-nine percent of pandemic influenza deaths occurred in people under sixty-five, and more than half in young adults twenty to forty years old.
- Between 2 and 20 percent of those infected by Spanish flu died, as opposed to the normal flu epidemic mortality rate of 0.1 percent.
- The very first case occurred on March 11 at Camp Funston, Kansas. An army cook named Albert Mitchell came down with flu symptoms that included a fever, sore throat, headache, and aching muscles. By noon 107 soldiers reported feeling similar symptoms. After two days, more than 500 were sick.
- In America, almost two hundred thousand people died from the flu in October 1918, making it the deadliest month in national history.
- On a single October day, 851 New Yorkers died from the flu.
- During the pandemic, residents of Philadelphia experienced death rates seven hundred times greater than normal.
- Outbreaks paralyzed nations in North America, Europe, Asia, Africa, Latin America, the South Pacific, and even the Arctic.
- Between 2.5 and 5 percent of the human population was wiped out.
- In India 17 million people died from the flu. This was about 5 percent of India's entire population.
- In Britain as many as 250,000 died.
- In France more than 400,000 died.
- In Canada approximately 50,000 died

- In Australia an estimated 12,000 people died.
- In the Fiji Islands, 14 percent of the population died in just two weeks.
- Sixty percent of the Eskimo population was wiped out in Alaska.
- Islander populations such as the Samoans suffered infection rates as high as 80 to 90 percent.
- Half of all U.S. soldiers who died in World War I succumbed to the Spanish flu, not to war wounds.
- More people died in one year from the 1918–1919 pandemic than in four years of the Black Death (bubonic plague) from 1347 to 1351.
- Influenza probably killed 25 million in its first twenty-five weeks; AIDS, by contrast, killed 25 million in its first twenty-five years.

Facts about avian influenza (bird flu):
- Avian influenza, known as "bird flu," is an infection caused by influenza viruses that occur naturally in birds.
- Wild birds can carry the viruses but usually do not get sick from them. However, some domesticated birds, including chickens, ducks, and turkeys, can become infected and die.
- One strain of avian influenza, the H5N1 virus, is prevalent in Asia and has spread to parts of Europe and Africa.
- Avian H5N1 infections have recently killed poultry and other birds in a number of countries.
- Strains of avian H5N1 influenza may infect various types of animals, including wild birds, pigs, and tigers.
- Human H5N1 influenza infection was first recognized in 1997 when it infected eighteen people in Hong Kong, killing six.
- Close contact with infected poultry has been the primary source for human infection.
- There have been isolated reports of human-to-human transmission of the virus.

- As of 2007, H5N1 has caused
  - 8 cases, 5 deaths in Azerbaijan
  - 7 cases, 7 deaths in Cambodia
  - 25 cases, 15 deaths in China
  - 1 case, 0 deaths in Djibouti
  - 36 cases, 15 deaths in Egypt
  - 100 cases, 80 deaths in Indonesia
  - 3 cases, 2 deaths in Iraq
  - 2 cases, 2 deaths in Laos
  - 1 case, 1 death in Nigeria
  - 25 cases, 17 deaths in Thailand
  - 12 cases, 4 deaths in Turkey
  - 90 cases, 42 deaths in Vietnam
  - 313 cases, 191 deaths total worldwide
- The reported symptoms of avian influenza in humans include fever, cough, sore throat, muscle aches, eye infections, acute respiratory distress, viral pneumonia, and severe life-threatening complications.
- Vaccines to protect humans against H5N1 viruses currently are under development. Two vaccines, called Tamiflu and Relenza, may be useful treatments for H5N1 avian influenza.

Opinion about pandemics:

According to a 2006 Harvard School of Public Health survey on pandemics:

- Sixty percent of Americans are concerned about bird flu.
- Of adults who have children, 44 percent think it "likely" or "somewhat likely" there will be "cases of bird flu among humans in the U.S. during the next 12 months."
- Less than 20 percent of respondents considered it "not at all" likely.
- Just 2 percent of Americans have talked to their doctor about flu vaccines or other antiviral medications.

- Forty-six percent of poll respondents who eat chicken said they would stop eating chicken out of concern for contracting bird flu.
- Seventy-five percent said if a pandemic broke out, they would reduce or avoid travel.
- Seventy-one percent said if a pandemic broke out, they would skip public events.
- Sixty-eight percent said if a pandemic broke out, they would stay home and keep their children at home while the outbreak lasted.

Finding and Using Sources of Information

No matter what type of essay you are writing, it is necessary to find information to support your point of view. You can use sources such as books, magazine articles, newspaper articles, and online articles.

Using Books and Articles

You can find books and articles in a library by using the library's computer or cataloging system. If you are not sure how to use these resources, ask a librarian to help you. You can also use a computer to find many magazine articles and other articles written specifically for the Internet.

You are likely to find a lot more information than you can possibly use in your essay, so your first task is to narrow it down to what is likely to be most usable. Look at book and article titles. Look at book chapter titles and examine the book's index to see if it contains information on the specific topic you want to write about. (For example, if you want to write about biofuels and you find a book about alternative energy sources, check the chapter titles and index to be sure it contains information about biofuels before you bother to check out the book.)

For a five-paragraph essay, you do not need a great deal of supporting information, so quickly try to narrow down your materials to a few good books and magazine or Internet articles. You do not need dozens. You might even find that one or two good books or articles contain all the information you need.

You probably do not have time to read an entire book, so find the chapters or sections that relate to your topic and skim these. When you find useful information, copy it onto a note card or into a notebook. You should look for supporting facts, statistics, quotations, and examples.

Using the Internet

When you select your supporting information, it is important that you evaluate its source. This is especially important with information you find on the Internet. Because nearly anyone can put information on the Internet, there is as much bad information as good information. Before using Internet information—or any information—try to determine if the source seems to be reliable. Is the author or Internet site sponsored by a legitimate organization? Is it from a government source? Does the author have any special knowledge or training relating to the topic you are looking up? Does the article give any indication of where its information comes from?

Using Your Supporting Information

When you use supporting information from a book, article, interview, or other source, there are three important things to remember:

1. *Make it clear whether you are using a direct quotation or a paraphrase.* If you copy information directly from your source, you are quoting it. You must put quotation marks around the information, and tell where the information comes from. If you put the information in your own words, you are paraphrasing it.

Here is an example of a using a quotation:
Fears that avian influenza will jump from birds to humans are unwarranted. As Professor Peter Curson says, "There is no evidence of the bird flu virus combining with the human flu virus or developing the ability to jump directly to human populations. Certainly the virus has been mutating, but this is not unusual in respiratory viruses."

Here is an example of a brief paraphrase of the same passage: Fears that avian influenza will jump from birds to humans are unwarranted. Many experts, such as Professor Peter Curson, say there is no evidence that bird flu has or will jump to human populations. While it is natural for viruses to mutate, there is no evidence—and thus no reason to suspect —the virus that sickens birds would mutate into something that would sicken people.

2. *Use the information fairly.* Be careful to use supporting information in the way the author intended it. For example, it is unfair to quote an author as saying, "Pandemics constitute one of the greatest threats to humankind," when he or she intended to say, "Pandemics constitute one of the greatest threats to humankind—they rank up there with reality television, Elmo, and Y2K." This is called taking information out of context. This is using supporting evidence unfairly.

3. *Give credit where credit is due.* Giving credit is known as citing. You must use citations when you use someone else's information, but not every piece of supporting information needs a citation.

   • If the supporting information is general knowledge—that is, it can be found in many sources —you do not have to cite your source.

   • If you directly quote a source, you must cite it.

   • If you paraphrase information from a specific source, you must cite it. If you do not use citations where you should, you are plagiarizing —or stealing—someone else's work.

Citing Your Sources

There are a number of ways to cite your sources. Your teacher will probably want you to do it in one of three ways:

- *Informal:* As in the example in number 1 above, tell where you got the information as you present it in the text of your essay.
- *Informal list:* At the end of your essay, place an un-numbered list of all the sources you used. This tells the reader where, in general, your information came from.
- *Formal:* Use numbered footnotes or endnotes. Footnotes or endnotes are generally placed at the end of an article or essay, although they may be placed elsewhere depending on your teacher's requirements.

Work Cited

Curson, Peter, "We're Suffering a Pandemic of Panic," *Sydney Morning Herald* 19 Jan. 2006.

Using MLA Style to Create a Works Cited List

You will probably need to create a list of works cited for your paper. These include materials that you quoted from, relied heavily on, or consulted to write your paper. There are several different ways to structure these references. The following examples are based on Modern Language Association (MLA) style, one of the major citation styles used by writers.

Book Entries

For most book entries you will need the author's name, the book's title, where it was published, what company published it, and the year it was published. This information is usually found on the inside of the book. Variations on book entries include the following:

A book by a single author:
Afrasiabi, Kaveh. *Iran's Nuclear Program: Debating Facts Versus Fiction.* Charleston, SC: BookSurge, 2006.

Two or more books by the same author:
Friedman, Thomas L. *From Beirut to Jerusalem.* New York: Doubleday, 1989.
—— *The World Is Flat: A Brief History of the Twentieth Century.* New York: Farrar, Straus and Giroux, 2005.

A book by two or more authors:
Pojman, Louis P., and Jeffrey Reiman. *The Death Penalty: For and Against.* Lanham, MD: Rowman & Littlefield, 1998.

A book with an editor:
Friedman, Lauri S., ed. *Introducing Issues with Opposing Viewpoints: Weapons of Mass Destruction.* Farmington Hills, MI: Greenhaven, 2006.

Periodical and Newspaper Entries

Entries for sources found in periodicals and newspapers are cited a bit differently from books. For one, these sources usually have a title and a publication name. They also may have specific dates and page numbers. Unlike book entries, you do not need to list where newspapers or periodicals are published or what company publishes them.

An article from a periodical:
> Zakaria, Fareed. "Let Them Eat Carrots." *Newsweek* 23 Oct. 2004: 42.

An unsigned article from a periodical:
> "Going Critical, Defying the World." Economist 21 Oct. 2004: 70.

An article from a newspaper:
> McCain, John. "The War You're Not Reading About." *Washington Post* 8 Apr. 2007: B07.

Internet Sources

To document a source you found online, try to provide as much information on it as possible, including the author's name, the title of the document, date of publication or of last revision, the URL, and your date of access.

A Web source:
> Shyovitz, David. "The History and Development of Yiddish." Jewish Virtual Library 30 May 2005 < www.jewishvirtuallibrary.org/jsource/History/yiddish. html >. Accessed September 4, 2007.

Your teacher will tell you exactly how information should be cited in your essay. Generally, the very least information needed is the original author's name and the name of the article or other publication.

Be sure you know exactly what information your teacher requires before you start looking for your supporting information so that you know what information to include with your notes.

Sample Essay Topics

For Expository Papers

A Look at the 1918 Pandemic

What Is a Pandemic?

What Is Avian Influenza?

Examining Diseases That Have the Potential to Become Pandemics

Exploring the Likelihood of a Pandemic

Pandemics Through History—Mild, Moderate, Severe

How to Respond to a Pandemic

How *Not* to Respond to a Pandemic

Separating Pandemic Panic from Reality

For Persuasive Papers

The World Is Overdue for a Pandemic

The World Is Not Overdue for a Pandemic

The World Is Not Prepared to Respond to a Pandemic

Hysteria over Pandemics Is Necessary to Raise Awareness About Them

Hysteria over Pandemics Erodes the Public's Trust in the Government

Fears About a Pandemic Are Justified

Fears About a Pandemic Are Overblown

A Bird Flu Pandemic Is Likely to Occur

A Bird Flu Pandemic Is Not Likely to Occur

AIDS Is a Pandemic

AIDS Is Not a Pandemic

Obesity Constitutes a Pandemic

Obesity Does Not Constitute a Pandemic

Avian Influenza Is Likely to Spread to Humans

Organizations to Contact

The editors have compiled the following list of organizations concerned with the issues debated in this book. The descriptions are derived from materials provided by the organizations. All have publications or information available for interested readers. The list was compiled on the date of publication of the present volume; names, addresses, and phone numbers may change. Be aware that many organizations take several weeks or longer to respond to inquiries, so allow as much time as possible.

AIDS Coalition to Unleash Power (ACT UP/New York)
332 Bleecker St., G5, New York, NY 10014
phone/fax: (212) 966-4873
e-mail: actupny@panix.com
Web site: www.actupny.org

ACT UP is a group of individuals committed to direct action to end the AIDS crisis. Through education and demonstrations, ACT UP works to end discrimination; achieve adequate funding for AIDS research, health care, and housing for people with AIDS; and disseminate information about safer sex, clean needles, and other AIDS prevention methods. ACT UP publishes action manuals, such as Time to Become an AIDS Activist, and online action reports.

Alliance for the Prudent Use of Antibiotics (APUA)
75 Kneeland St., Boston, MA 02111-1901
(617) 636-0966
e-mail: apua@tufts.edu • Web site: www.tufts.edu/med/apua/

The alliance is a grassroots organization dedicated to research and education about appropriate antibiotic use.

By advocating the prudent use of antibiotics, the APUA seeks to preserve the power of antibiotics by preventing the increase of pathogens' resistance to them. APUA publishes information pamphlets, a newsletter, and the video *Confronting Antibiotic Resistance: An Increasing Threat to Public Health.*

American Council on Science and Health (ACSH)

1995 Broadway, 2nd Fl., New York, NY 10023-5860
(212) 362-7044 • fax: (212) 362-4919
e-mail: acsh@acsh.org • Web site: www.acsh.org

ACSH is a consumer education group concerned with issues related to food, nutrition, chemicals, pharmaceuticals, lifestyle, the environment, and health. It publishes several fact sheets and papers about pandemics, including "Avian Influenza, or 'Bird Flu': What You Need to Know," and "Don't Worry About the Flu . . . at Least, Not the 1957 Type."

American Medical Association (AMA)

515 N. State St., Chicago, IL 60610
(800) 621-8335
Web site: www.ama-assn.org

AMA is the largest professional association for medical doctors. It helps set standards for medical education and practices, and it is a powerful lobby in Washington for physicians' interests. The association publishes journals for many medical fields, including the monthly *Archives of Surgery* and the weekly *JAMA*. Its Web site offers papers on subjects relating to preparing for and preventing pandemic outbreaks.

American Public Health Association (APHA)

800 I St. NW, Washington, DC 20001-3710
(202) 777-APHA • fax: (202) 777-2534
e-mail: comments@apha.org • Web site: www.apha.org

Founded in 1872, the American Public Health Association consists of over fifty thousand individuals and organizations that aim to improve public health. Its members represent over fifty public health occupations, including researchers, practitioners, administrators, teachers, and other health care workers. Some of APHA's publications include the monthly *American Journal of Public Health* and several papers, newsletters, and updates devoted to issues related to pandemics, and avian influenza in particular.

Center for Infectious Disease Research and Policy (CIDRAP)

University of Minnesota Academic Health Center
420 Delaware St., SE MMC 263
Minneapolis, MN 55455
(612) 626-6770
e-mail: cidrap@umn.edu • Web site: www.cidrap.umn.edu/index.html

CIRDAP's mission is to prevent illness and death from infectious diseases through epidemiologic research and the rapid translation of scientific information into real-world practical applications and solutions. It provides a wealth of information on infectious diseases that could become pandemics, such as avian influenza, seasonal influenza, and deadly pathogens that could be released in a bioterrorist attack.

Center for Science in the Public Interest (CSPI)

1875 Connecticut Ave. NW, Suite 300
Washington, DC 20009
(202) 332-9110 • fax: (202) 265-4954
e-mail: cspi@cspinet.org • Web site: www.cspinet.org

The center is a nonprofit education and advocacy organization that focuses on improving the safety and nutritional quality of America's food supply. The CSPI educates the public about nutrition and lobbies for food safety regulation in an attempt to avoid public health crises. It publishes the *Nutrition Action Healthletter* and organizes grassroots campaigns for food labeling and safety. Its publications relating to pandemics include *First Ministering to the Sick* and *Outbreak Alert*.

Centers for Disease Control and Prevention

4770 Buford Hwy., Mailstop K28
Atlanta, GA 30341-3724
(770) 488-3235 • fax: (770) 488-3236
e-mail: genetics@cdc.gov • Web site:
www.cdc.gov/flu/avian

The Centers for Disease Control and Prevention is a government organization concerned with preventing and controlling outbreaks of disease. Its department on pandemics offers a plethora of fact sheets, time lines, news updates, and background information on bird flu, swine flu, seasonal flu, and other pandemic topics. Free reports are available for downloading, including *Ethical Guidelines for Pandemic Influenza*.

Federation of American Scientists—Program for Monitoring Emerging Diseases (ProMED)

1717 K St. NW, Suite 209, Washington, DC 20036
(202) 546-3300
e-mail: dpreslar@fas.org • Web site:
www.fas.org/promed

The Federation of American Scientists is a privately funded, nonprofit organization engaged in analysis and advocacy on science, technology, and public policy for global security. ProMED seeks to link scientists, public health officials, journalists, and laypersons in a global communications network for reporting disease outbreaks. The federation requests that students and other researchers first investigate the resources available on its Web site, such as the papers "Controlling Infectious Diseases" and "Global Monitoring of Emerging Diseases: Design for a Demonstration Program," before requesting further information.

HIV/AIDS Treatment Information Service (ATIS)
PO Box 6303, Rockville, MD 20849-6303
(800) HIV-0440 (800-448-0440) • fax: (301) 519-6616
e-mail: atis@hivatis.org • Web site: www.hivatis.org

ATIS provides information about federally approved treatment guidelines for HIV and AIDS. It publishes *Principles of Therapy of HIV Infection* as well as reports and guidelines for treating HIV infection in adults, adolescents, and children.

National AIDS Fund
729 Fifteenth Street NW, 9th Floor
Washington, DC 20005-1511
(202) 408-4848 • fax: (202) 408-1818
e-mail: info@aidsfund.org • Web site:
www.aidsfund.org

The National AIDS Fund seeks to eliminate HIV as a major health and social problem. Its members work in partnership with the public and private sectors to provide care and to prevent new infections in communities and in the workplace by means of advocacy, grants, research, and education. The fund publishes the monthly newsletter *News from the National AIDS Fund*.

National Coalition on Health Care
1200 G Street NW, Suite 750, Washington, DC 20005
(202) 638-7151
e-mail: info@nchc.org • Web site: www.nchc.org

The National Coalition on Health Care is a nonprofit, nonpartisan group that represents the nation's largest alliance working to improve America's health care and make it more affordable. The coalition offers several policy studies with titles ranging from *Why the Quality of U.S. Health Care Must Be Improved* to *The Rising Number of Uninsured Workers: An Approaching Crisis in Health Care Financing*. It occasionally publishes reports on how to strengthen the health care system in the event of a pandemic outbreak.

National Foundation for Infectious Diseases

4733 Bethesda Ave., Suite 750, Bethesda, MD 20814
(301) 656-0003 • fax: (301) 907-0878
e-mail: nfid@aol.com • Web site: www.nfid.org

The foundation is a nonprofit philanthropic organization
that supports disease research through grants and fel-
lowships and educates the public about research, treatment, and prevention of infectious diseases, including
AIDS. It publishes a newsletter, *Double Helix*, and its Web
site contains a "Virtual Library of Diseases."

National Institute of Allergy and Infectious Diseases (NIAID)

6610 Rockledge Dr., MSC-6612
Bethesda, MD 20892-6612
Web site: www.niaid.nih.gov

The institute, one of the programs of the National
Institutes of Health, supports scientists conducting
research on infectious, immunologic, and allergic diseases that afflict people worldwide. Emerging diseases,
pandemics, and AIDS constitute just a few of NIAID's
main areas of research, and many materials are available from NIAID on these topics.

National Institutes of Health (NIH)

9000 Rockville Pike, Bethesda, MD 20892
(301) 496-4000
e-mail: NIHinfo@od.nih.gov • Web site: www.nih.gov

The NIH is made up of twenty-seven separate components, including the National Human Genome Research
Institute and the National Cancer Institute. Its mission is
to discover new knowledge that will improve everyone's
health. In order to achieve this mission, the NIH conducts
and supports research, helps train research investiga-
tors, and fosters the communication of medical information. The NIH also publishes online fact sheets, brochures,
and handbooks, many on topics related to pandemics.

National Vaccine Information Center
204 Mill St., Suite B1, Vienna, VA 22180
(703) 938-0342
e-mail: info@909shot.com • Web site:
www.909shot.com

The center is dedicated to the prevention of vaccine injuries and deaths through public education. It is operated by Dissatisfied Parents Together, a national nonprofit educational organization that advocates reforming the mass vaccination system. The center distributes information on vaccine safety and on reporting adverse effects after vaccination.

U.S. Department of Health and Human Services (HHS) Interagency Public Affairs
Group on Influenza Preparedness and Response
200 Independence Ave. SW, Washington, DC 20201
(800) 232-4636
e-mail: cdcinfo@cdc.gov • Web site:
www.pandemicflu.gov

A wing of the Department of Health and Human Services that provides comprehensive government-wide information on pandemic influenza and avian influenza for the general public, health and emergency preparedness professionals, policy makers, government and business leaders, school systems, and local communities.

World Health Organization (WHO)
Avenue Appia 20
CH - 1211 Geneva 27
Switzerland
+ 41 22 791 2111
Web site: www.who.int

The WHO is the directing and coordinating authority for health within the United Nations system. It is responsible for providing leadership on global health matters, shaping the health research agenda, setting norms and standards, articulating evidence-based policy options, providing technical support to countries, and monitoring and assessing health trends. The WHO has a special department devoted to avian influenza, through which it publishes fact sheets and articles about bird flu and other issues related to pandemics.

Bibliography

Books

Barry, John M., *The Great Influenza: The Story of the Deadliest Pandemic in History*. New York: Penguin, 2005.

Bongmba, Elias Kifon, *Facing a Pandemic: The African Church and the Crisis of Aids*. Waco, TX: Baylor University Press, 2007.

Crosby, Alfred W., *America's Forgotten Pandemic: The Influenza of 1918*. Cambridge: Cambridge University Press, 2003.

Johnson, Joan J., and William E. Rose. *Pandemic*. Charleston: BookSurge, 2005.

Kalla, Daniel, *Pandemic*. New York: Forge, 2005.

Knobler, Stacey L., Alison Mack, and Adel Mahmoud, eds. *Threat of Pandemic Influenza: Are We Ready?* Washington, DC: Institute of Medicine, March 2005.

Selzer, Michael I., *The Coming Avian Flu Pandemic*. South Egremont, MA: Farshaw, 2006.

Siegel, Marc K., *Bird Flu: Everything You Need to Know About the Next Pandemic*. Hoboken, NJ: Wiley, 2006.

Smallman, Shawn, *The AIDS Pandemic in Latin America*. Chapel Hill, NC: University of North Carolina Press, 2007.

Periodicals

Abercrombie, George, "Avian Flu Pandemic Would Not Be a Typical Emergency." *Los Angeles Business Journal*, 23 Apr. 2007: 67.

Bush, George W., "President Outlines Pandemic Influenza Preparations and Response." The White House 1 Nov. 2005 < www.whitehouse.gov/news/releases/2005/11/20051101-1.html > .

Curson, Peter, "We're Suffering a Pandemic of Panic." *Sydney Morning Herald*, 19 Jan. 2006.

"FDA Pandemic Influenza Preparedness Strategic Plan," U.S. Department of Heath and Human Services, Food and Drug Administration, 14 Mar. 2007 < www. fda. gov/oc/op/pandemic/strategicplan03_07.html > .

Fekete, Thomas, "Avian Flu Explained." *Toronto Daily News*, 2006.

Fitzpatrick, Michael, "Pandemic Flu: Turning a Drama into a Crisis." *Spiked*, 25 Nov. 2005 < www.spiked-online. com/Articles/0000000CAE8A.htm > .

Fitzpatrick, Mike, "The Pandemic Flu Panic." *British Journal of General Practice*, 1 May 2006: 389.

Fumento, Michael, "Fuss and Feathers: Pandemic Panic over the Avian Flu," *Weekly Standard*, 21 Nov. 2005.

Garrett, Laurie, "The Next Pandemic?" *Foreign Affairs*, July/Aug. 2005.

Harris, Richard, "U.S. Plan to Stockpile Bird-Flu Vaccine a Big Gamble." National Public Radio, 6 Jan. 2006 < www.npr.org/templates/story.php?storyId = 5133306 > .

Highfield, Roger, "A Flu Pandemic Is Long Overdue." *Telegraph* [London], 21 Feb. 2006.

Jakab, Zsuzsanna, "Putting the Risk to Human Health from Bird Flu (type A/H5N1) in Perspective," European Center for Disease Prevention and Control, 2005.

Levy, Sue-Ann, "Flu Crisis or Empire Building?" *Toronto Sun*, 10 May 2005.

Mackenzie, Debora, "Can Tamiflu Save Us from Bird Flu?" New Scientist.com 2 June 2005 < www.newscientist. com/article/mg18625023.100.html > .

Markel, Howard, "The Flu Snafu—the Story Behind Strain A (H2N2)." *Globalist*, 18 Apr. 2005 < www.theglobal ist. com/dbweb/StoryId.aspx?StoryId = 4502 > .

Oxford, John, "We Can't Afford to Be Caught Napping Again." *Times* [London], 20 Oct. 2005

Ross, Gilbert, "Science Is Not a Democracy." *Washington Times*, 15 June 2007.

Seavey, Todd, "Two Paths Away from Pandemic: A Vaccine and Tamiflu May Ward Off Bird Flu." *American Council on Science and Health*, 9 Aug. 2005.

Soronen, Lisa E., Address to the National Academies, Institute of Medicine, Committee on Modeling Community Containment for Pandemic Influenza, 26 Oct. 2006 < www.nsba.org/site/docs/39600/39528.pdf > .

Steer, Jen, "Bird Flu Pandemic Won't Pan Out." *Daily Kent Stater*, 9 Dec. 2005.

Stimola, Aubrey Noelle, "Avian Influenza, or 'Bird Flu': What You Need to Know." *American Council on Science and Health*, 9 Mar. 2006 < www.acsh.org/docLib/20060309-birdflu.pdf > .

Stipp, David, "Is the Risk Overblown? Calling a Pandemic 'Overdue' Is a Misnomer Worthy of Chicken Little." *Fortune Magazine*, 7 Mar. 2005.

Woodward, Nancy Hatch, "Pandemic." Society for Human Resource Management. *HR*, May 2006.

Web Sites

The American Experience: Influenza 1918 (www.pbs.org/wgbh/amex/influenza). A comprehsive Web site about the effects of the 1918–1919 influenza pandemic in the United States. Contains time line, maps, and a special teacher's guide.

Avian Influenza (www.fao.org/avianflu/en/index.html). This site, maintained by the Food and Agriculture Organization of the United Nations, provides useful background and news updates on avian influenza. Colorful graphics such as maps and charts make it easy to follow outbreaks around the world.

CIDRAP (www.cidrap.unm.edu/). Headquartered at the University of Minnesota, the Center for Infectious Disease Research and Policy's Web site (CIDRAP) has breaking news updates regarding pandemics.

Pandemic Flu and You—Get Prepared (www.pandemicfluandyou.org/). Sponsored by the Pew Charitable Trusts, this helpful Web site provides pandemic information on a state-by-state basis. It also contains links to breaking news items related to pandemics.

Pandemic Flu.gov (www.pandemicflu.gov). An arm of the Department of Health and Human Services that provides comprehensive government-wide information on pandemic influenza and avian influenza for the general public, health and emergency preparedness professionals, policy makers, government and business leaders, school systems, and local communities.

World Health Organization's Avian Influenza Page (www.who.int/csr/disease/avian-influenza/en/). The World Health Organization is responsible for coordinating the global response to human cases of H5N1 avian influenza and monitoring the corresponding threat of an influenza pandemic. Its Web site tracks the evolving situation and provides access to both technical guidelines and information useful to the general public.

Index

Tumpey, Terrence, 66

U
Uncertainty, 29
United States, 10, 17–19, 37
Uyeki, Tim, 62

V
Vaccines, 58
  changes in, 34
  development of, 38, 48, 57

planning for needed, 56–57
as preventive measure, 44
research on, 52
shortages of, 53–54, 62
Ventilators, 54
Vietnam, 47

W
Webster, Robert, 42
World Health Organization (WHO), 36, 62, 64

Picture Credits

Maury Aaseng, 19, 24, 35, 43, 55

AP Images, 10, 13, 16, 21, 27, 28, 33, 38, 41, 46, 53, 58, 63, 66

©2006 Wright, The Detroit News, and Politicalcartoons.com, 44

About the Editor

Lauri S. Friedman earned her bachelor's degree in religion and political science from Vassar College in Poughkeepsie, New York. Her studies there focused on political Islam. Friedman has worked as a nonfiction writer, a newspaper journalist, and an editor for more than seven years. She has accumulated extensive experience in both academic and professional settings.

Friedman has edited and authored numerous publications for Greenhaven Press on controversial social issues such as gay marriage, Islam, energy, discrimination, suicide bombers, and the war on terror. Much of the Writing the Critical Essay series has been under her direction or authorship. She was instrumental in the creation of the series and played a critical role in its conception and development.